# LITTLE DEATH



*NEW YORK TIMES & USA TODAY* BESTSELLING AUTHOR

## NICOLE BLANCHARD

# DEDICATION

*To you freaks who want*
*to be chased by a psychopath,*
*turn the page...*

# GOOD GIRL

*Now run.*

# CONTENTS

# TRIGGER WARNINGS

Little Death is a dark romance novella featuring an indecent proposal from an irresistible psychopath. As such, please mind the following warnings:

Degradation
Humiliation
Gun Play
Mask Play
Blood Play
Pierced Hero
Spanking
Coercion
Morally grey heroine
Morally black hero
Obsessive Behavior / Stalking
Murder
Organized Crime
Uneven Power Exchange
Emotional / Psychological Manipulation
Graphic Sexual Content
Improper use of masks
Dubious Consent

Please mind the triggers and take care of yourselves. - Nicole

# LITTLE DEATH PLAYLIST

One of the first things I do before I start writing is to create a playlist that I listen to while I write. Scan / click the QR code to listen along.

# CHAPTER ONE

The house glitters, filled with life, but all I see when I take it in is death.

It's the night before Halloween and I'm too old to be afraid of the dark, but that doesn't stop the hair at my nape from prickling as I move through the shadows to my destination. Too many horror movie marathons in the past several weeks have gotten to me. The screaming. The blood. My nightmares have been running rampant, and not even the sleeping pills my doctor prescribed are touching it.

So much for exposure therapy.

Freezing on the steps outside, as I look up at the grand facade of dusty-blue French Provincial double doors, I'm both comforted and disquieted by its familiar-ity. Wondering if this is the moment when a rational voice will save me from what I'm about to do. It's nothing like I'd imagine the gates of hell would resemble, but it sure feels like I'm about to walk into the devil's lair.

A humid October breeze, thick with the scent of sweet olive trees and spicy purple dianthus, whips around my freshly waxed legs and teases my nose. As I hesitate one moment longer, the rational voice in my head is glaringly absent. I'm alone, and the only voices present are those raised in drunken laughter, carried on the night air from the roaring party in the expansive gardens behind the estate. The sense of unreality reminds me of a carnival, sending a blaze of apprehension over me.

I suppose rationality died that day six months ago, and no amount of wishing will bring it back. It sure as hell seems like the more I cling to the tenuous bits of control I used to have, the more they seem to evaporate straight from my grasp.

Gathering my nerves, I tuck them away behind a perfected veil of calm. I straighten my shoulders, then breathe in until my pulse stops jumping and my nervous stomach settles. The glittery gold mask covering most of my face helps. With it, no one recognizes me. No one can placate me with false condolences or suffocate me with their blatant curiosity. I can be anyone but me.

Anonymity is fleeting when you're the daughter of a

well known local figure, and more so when your beloved mother commits suicide with you in the very home standing in front of me.

I gulp, shoving those memories away and knocking on the door with more force than necessary. A young man with pleasantly nondescript features answers, the cacophony of music, laughter, and conversation swelling around him. "Welcome. May I have your invitation?" His black Venetian mask glints under the porch lights as I pass it over to his waiting hand.

A glance behind him as he studies the invitation reveals more discreet staff in matching black tuxedos, the women in sleek black dresses, each carrying silver trays of fizzing drinks and *hors d'oeuvres*. My stomach retches in protest at the sight of food, and I inhale through my mouth. The staggering, opulent setting no longer strikes me as beautiful and pristine the way it used to. Now all I see is the carnage behind its mask.

The man clears his throat, eyes glued to mine as though he doesn't want to chance looking down. A spark of pleasure washes away my nerves, and I give myself a mental pat on the back for taking Yasmine's advice and choosing this dress. The perfect distraction. It's as short as sin, with a plunging V-neck and generous cut-outs at the sides and back that tease the dimples near my spine. Crafted in shimmering gold fringe at the bottom and a woven metallic gold at the bust, it matches my ornate gold and ceramic mask as though they were made for each other. It's not my normal pink ensembles, but the less I look like my usual self, the better.

My breath catches in my chest as he scans the name, but he barely reads it before checking it against a list on a clipboard. "Thank you," he says briskly, returning the invitation to me. *Senator Rory Gallagher & Family* is written across the front in elegant gold calligraphy. I send my dear old dad a mental thanks. It's the one and only time I've ever used his name to literally open doors for me.

"Have a lovely evening. The main gathering is through the living space and continues on the terrace and gardens for the charity games."

I murmur my thanks as I step inside, but I'm not sure my voice is loud enough for him to hear over the music from the string quartet on the other side of the patio doors. Oxygen clogs in my throat as a lifetime's worth of memories assault me the moment he closes us inside to await the next guest. It feels like home and, at the same time, wholly alien.

My gaze snaps to the grand curving staircase despite several pointed reminders on the way up here to stop myself from doing exactly that. But it's like I don't have control over my body. The entryway used to be my favorite part of the estate. The staircase, dominating most of the room, is a glorious feat of engineering, sweeping in a circle overhead and accented by scrolling, handcrafted ironwork.

After the night when I found my mother at the bottom, her body twisted into a gruesome knot and steeped in blood, the sight of those stairs makes my stomach heave all over again.

*Focus, Catriona.*

I give myself a little shake, as though it'll cement resolve into my brain. I can't afford to be distracted, not when this party is the only chance I may get to be in this house again. At the first opportunity, I ditch the invitation in one one of the trashcans placed strategically throughout the area. With a lump the size of a fist lodged in my throat, I smile beneath my mask and accept a glass of bubbling champagne from a passing server. The fizz dissolves my nerves, and I sip to have something to do with my hands while I study the surrounding faces. A buzz would help dispel the swelling apprehension hovering on the edges of my awareness.

My phone rings with a text from my oversized clutch. Squeezing between a potted plant and a man who doesn't understand the concept of getting the hell out of someone's way, I dig between a battery bank and condoms—Jesus Christ, Yasmine—for my phone. The man smiles from behind his devil mask when I'm forced to brush against him. I glare and let my champagne accidentally splash onto his Ralph Lauren suit.

"Oops," I say flatly.

His muttered, "Bitch," follows me as I stride through the entryway to the massive, open-concept formal living room, decorated in untouchable white furniture. I guess the new owner didn't care to redecorate. Everything is almost exactly as we had left it. Even the lovingly restored Steinway Model O that had belonged to my mother's father. Not that I knew him. All four of my grandparents were long since dead when I came into the picture. The ghost of a memory—my mother seated at the piano, plucking at the keys—threatens to rise to the surface of my thoughts, but I stifle it, turning away from the piano and opening my texts as soon as no one is around.

**Yasmine**
It's been 32 minutes. You promised you'd check in every half hour. Are you still alive? Do I need to send an ambulance? Reinforcements?

**Yasmine**
I had rounds until midnight. I should be asleep rn instead of stalking your location. I'm adding endless margs to the list of shit you owe me for putting me through this.

By reinforcements, she means her older brother Reggie, who is a police officer with the New Orleans PD. The last thing I need is for her to call the cops, and she knows it. Reggie may not be my brother, but he wouldn't hesitate to act like he was if Yasmine informed him about what I'm up to.

> I'm alive. Just got inside. I wish you were here

> **Yasmine**
> Oh, sure, because crashing a party thrown by NOLA's newest multibillionaire sounds like a good time to me.

Yasmine, bless her heart, is a better person than I am. She's also a much more trusting person than I am because she was raised by parents who believe in the premise of law and order. As lawyers, they have faith that our justice system, while flawed, will always do what's best. Over the last six months, I've had the unfortunate experience of being introduced to a different justice system. One that doesn't care about the facts, only closing cases. I don't believe anyone has my mother's best interests at heart. Especially since even those close to me—to her—aren't willing to do what needs to be done to find the truth.

The champagne is amazing

**Yasmine**
At least I know it's really you and not someone posing as you to cover up your murder. Have you seen him yet?

By him, she means the man of the hour and host of the party. Aiden O'Connor. The mysterious bastard who swept in when my family was vulnerable to buy my mother's ancestral estate in cash. It happened so fast after my mother died that I didn't even have time to lodge any protests with my father or figure out another move.

*I can't handle living in this house for another day, Catriona. Please don't make me feel any guiltier than I already do. It's too hard,* he'd said when he broke the news to us less than a month after her death. My younger sister, Elizabeth, had been too numb from the loss to take my side, and neither of them wanted to listen to my desperate pleas that Mom never would have committed suicide. She would never have left me behind. They wanted the whole ugly mess swept under the rug, perfectly content to accept the suicide findings from the police despite my testimony to the contrary.

We'd been staying in a hotel at the time, waiting for hazmat crews who specialize in renovations after incidents like this to clean the marble or replace it or whatever the hell they do. The blood had been... my stomach drops, and I flick the memory away. Anyway, it wasn't long after my father had announced the sale, hired moving crews, and within days, my mother's home—her pride and joy—was gone. Her legacy had been signed over to a stranger. It had taken me this long to find out who he sold it to because there was so little online about Aiden O'Connor. The enigmatic billionaire entrepreneur from Ireland has next to nothing on social media.

Seriously, what sort of psycho doesn't even have an Instagram account?

Remembering Yasmine, I type out a reply while studying my surroundings for a glimpse at the man in question. It's not why I'm here, but I can't stop myself. Who would want to buy the home where a famous socialite supposedly committed suicide?

Not yet, but I just got here.

As though the words conjure him to life, Aiden O'Connor appears in the hall, sycophants swarming at both sides. My hand loosens on my phone and the glass of champagne I'm still holding, almost sending them both careening to the floor, but I maintain my grip at the last second.

I recognize him from the lone picture I found. I'd studied it in rage for hours, so there's no way I'd miss him. I don't hear what the people around him are saying because a swell from the band drowns out the words, but I don't care. I don't need to hear anything. Seeing him is enough to make me want to leave without accomplishing a damn thing I set out to do.

Without realizing it, my feet have transported me backward into the doorway leading to the terrace. Most of the partygoers are there, hovering around the blackjack and craps tables, dressed in gaudy gowns and ornate tuxes that remind me of Mardi Gras. Their expressions are hungry behind their masks, eagerly awaiting the start of the gambling. People with money sure do love to play games with it. My back smacks into the doorframe, but I barely feel a thing. Masked faces blur around me, a funhouse of raucous laughter and devilry.

It's golden hour, the perfect time for an arc of waning sunlight to streak through the floor-to-ceiling windows and surround him in a brilliant halo. Like he's a fallen angel. His sinner's mouth, so full and tempting, is like art as it forms a response, but there's a buzzing in my ears drowning it out. My vision narrows until I see only him. If we were in a rom-com, this would be our meet-cute, but it's a jump scare instead.

His tailored black suit clings to his muscular body,

accentuating his broad shoulders, trim waist, and thick thighs. A snowy-white button-up strains over well-toned pectorals and parts at his neck, revealing a wealth of tattoos. The only one I can discern at a distance is a death moth at the base of his throat. The rest are shadows of ink—all black—that cover every available surface aside from his face. The fingers of one hand, covered in rings, dance as he twists a lone black and gold casino chip around his knuckles. He prowls through his admirers, a ready smile on his lips, but it doesn't quite reach his stormy gaze.

It's been a long time since I could tear my attention away to note that two men are on his heels. One is dressed in an understated black suit, similar to the one worn by the attendant at the front door. A quick study dismisses him as an assistant or bodyguard, maybe? He sticks to the background, eyes attentive, and rejects offers of champagne to murmur into an earbud he touches every few seconds like it doesn't fit quite right.

The other must be one of O'Connor's friends, because he sticks close to his side. His wide, manic smile is a ready punctuation to whatever he whispers in O'Connor's ear. He's dressed much more casually in a pair of black pants and an untucked white button-up, only halfway fastened, at best. A variety of gold chains adorn his neck and hang over the sleek muscles of his exposed chest. His hands frequently dive into dark, riotous curls, making them a wild mess around his angular, striking face. Even more striking are his impossibly light blue-green eyes.

To ease the ache in my stomach, I polish off the rest of my champagne and divert my focus. A ready server is nearby, appearing as though out of nowhere, and replenishes my glass with only a smile. I should pace myself—I'm going to need a clear head for what I have planned—but I down it in several long gulps.

When the fuzziness and warmth of the alcohol melt away my nerves, I look up and freeze.

Because Aiden O'Connor glares right back at me from beneath a blank white half-mask, his heavy brows furrowed, silver eyes piercing.

Staring at me like he knows I shouldn't be here.

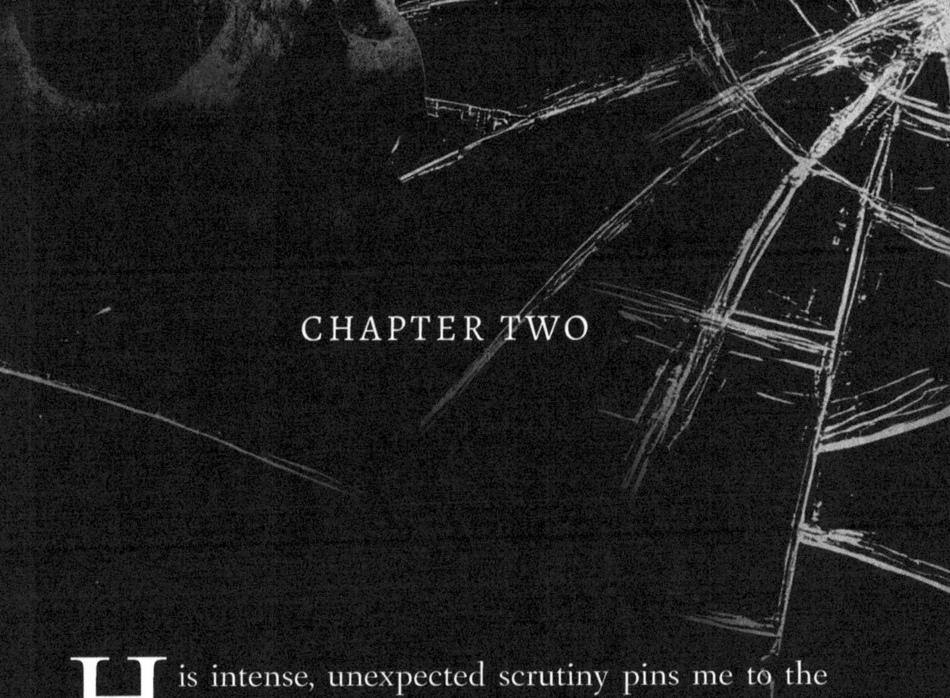

# CHAPTER TWO

His intense, unexpected scrutiny pins me to the spot. It can't last for more than a few heartbeats, but it feels like a century. Maybe he's trying to place me among his dozens of guests. Maybe he's wondering why I'm gaping at him. Either way, the line between his brow smooths away, and I question if it was ever there in the first place. One of his companions says something to him, and he angles his body away from me.

I unfreeze, my breath wheezing from my lungs like his attention had been a weight pressing on my chest. Soon, but not soon enough, he and his entourage move through the door next to me. He's so close for a moment, the scent of him teases my nose. Silly, because it could be either of the men at his side, but somehow, I know the dark, earthy aroma belongs to him.

The last thing I want to do is draw any attention to myself, so I wander a few steps away to admire the pamphlets detailing today's charity event with several of the other guests. My heart continues its frantic fluttering until the three men are through the door and out of sight.

> I knew you were a witch. Did you summon him? He just looked right at me. I think I had a heart attack.

> **Yasmine**
> I picked a terrible time to be a lapsed Catholic. I thought you were going to stay as far away from him as possible??????

The squeal of feedback from a microphone cuts through the string quartet, and a clear, feminine voice comes through over hidden speakers I know are present throughout the living spaces. I use the distraction to weave through the crowd, but it's nearly impossible because the guests are making their way en masse to the terrace doors.

"On behalf of the Emerald Isle staff, we'd like to welcome you to our charity gala to support our grand opening next week. As you all know, all proceeds from tonight's event will be donated to support the New Orleans Regional Hospital. I'm here to introduce the man of the evening, Mr. Aiden O'Connor! Let's give him a hand!"

Polite applause punctuates the introduction, followed by Aiden's throaty growl, and I hide my seething expression behind another gulp of champagne. "Thank you." He says you like ye, and I scoff inwardly at his undeniably attractive Irish accent. "And thank you for bein' here tonight to support this new venture and raise some money for a good cause. That means it's time to open those pocketbooks and find your inner generosity. The O'Connor Foundation plans to match every dollar."

A glance around shows everyone riveted by this proclamation. It's impressive, that's for sure. But I don't buy a word of it.

Me: I wasn't looking for him. He was going outside, and I was in his way.

Yasmine: Should I go back to church? My mom will be thrilled, so that's one reason not to go. But I'm willing to do this for your wayward soul.

Me: No?

Yasmine: ...so is he hot?

Me: No!

Yasmine: I knew it. He's fine as hell, isn't he?

Abandoning my empty champagne glass with a nearby server and declining a refill, I move to the window next to the piano and find Aiden instantly at a makeshift stage, surrounded by a ring of guests. Even at a distance, he has a commanding presence...and a beautiful one. I'd called him a fallen angel, and the same description comes to me again as he continues his speech. From his gorgeous face to his dark golden hair, the people gazing up at him look like they'd follow him to hell at the slightest provocation.

I turn away from the sight and push him from my thoughts. He doesn't matter, and I'll probably never see him again. The main room is almost empty, so it's the perfect time for me to make my escape and put my plan into motion.

Me: No.

I don't need to see her face to know she's probably calling me a liar.

The only picture I could find must have been taken when he was much younger. Before he inherited his father's millions, and started his hospitality empire. According to the limited information available, he used his inheritance to open his first casino in Ireland. It was wildly successful, leading him to replicate the same approach in several European countries and ultimately expand into America.

> Yasmine: Liar. Please don't let his devilish good looks distract you. I won't survive medical school without you if you get caught and sent to jail for trespassing.

Moving toward the stairs requires me to weave through the stragglers on their way to the terrace, lured by the siren call of Aiden's Irish brogue. My ready excuse is that I got lost in the maze of a mansion in my search for a bathroom. No one will question that because I don't plan to take this mask off until I'm safely back home. Little do they know, I used to be the princess of this castle.

> Me: Don't worry. He's distracted playing host. I'm going up while everyone is outside. It'll be fine. In and out.

> Yasmine: The fact that you think any part of this is fine is what tells me it's a terrible idea. Don't say I didn't warn you.

Me: I'll text you again in 30 when I'm out of here and safe. You worry too much.

Yasmine: I'm going to steal meds from the hospital to sedate myself.

Me: Love you too!

I never thought I'd do many things six months ago. Struggling through law school is one. Sneaking around a party thrown by New Orleans' newest billionaire is another.

But I'm not the same person I was six months ago.

That person died along with my mother.

I take the stairs as quickly as I dare to avoid capturing attention, but it doesn't seem to matter. The waitstaff is too busy clearing away forgotten drinks and appetizers to pay me any attention. The thought of my mother's ghost and replaying morbid thoughts keeps me moving at a fast clip until I reach the top.

My goal is at the farthest end of the hallway, a spare room my mother had turned into a library slash hideaway for herself. If I'm going to find her phone—the last possible vestige of clues about what happened to her—that's the only place it could be. After her death, my father says he and the police searched high and low for it, but they never found it. If I'm wrong and her death was an accident, there'll be nothing on it, and I'll give up my crusade...but if I'm right...If I'm right, it'll be the proof I need to make the police and my father take my concerns seriously.

Every few steps, I glance behind me, certain someone will be close on my heels, but I see nothing but my shadow. It doesn't stop my heart from galloping or the sweat from beading on my hairline. Swiping at it nervously, I stamp out the first blooms of hope that make my hand shake as I reach for the door handle.

It doesn't turn.

Fuck.

Cursing some more under my breath, I break out a small pack of hot-pink tools from my clutch—thank God I packed them and opted for the bigger purse—and get to work. As I fumble with the tools, I hope the YouTube videos I watched will be enough to break in. On my third try, miraculously, the lock pops open, and I throw myself inside with a muffled squeak of surprise.

The scent hits me like a tackle from a linebacker, stopping me mid-stride, and I slap a hand over my mouth and nose to mask it. My other hand grips the doorframe to keep myself upright. A cold weight plops into my stomach. Each inhale draws in more of my mother's Dior perfume until I could swear she's present in the room with me. Not even the scent of fresh paint drowns it out.

When I gather my wits and crack my eyes open, however, no one is in the room but me. The shelves where she'd curated her beloved mystery novels are bare, save for bland masculine decor. They've been painted a glossy black, which I immediately despise on principle. Instead of her comfortable antique reading chairs and Tiffany lamps, there's a sleek, expensive-looking pool table. A rack of cues lines the wall to my left. Her neutral blue-green walls have been covered over with more black.

My heels catch on the Oriental rug as I practically sprint across the room to the window seat on the far wall. Flinging the compartment open, I find the storage space underneath empty aside from spare pillows, but that doesn't deter me. When we were younger, Elizabeth and I discovered a hidden compartment inside. We used it to pass notes to Mom or each other. Mom would surprise us with gifts—little things to show she was thinking of us. Candy. Books. Toys. Trinkets from her travels.

Memories flood me of the thousands of times I've done this before. The back of my throat closes, nose stinging. My hand trembles uncontrollably as I reach to dislodge the panel to the secret compartment. I hesitate for the slightest moment before I apply pressure. My chest cracks open along with the panel door. Quickly, I reach inside and feel blindly around, half dreading I'll find nothing, half afraid of what I will find.

If there's nothing, then this wild, crazed feeling I've been living with will simply be grief. It's been hell, but at least I'll know the truth. At least it will give me the impetus to deal with it. If there's nothing there, it'll be the first step to accepting she'd been a deeply unhappy woman who'd chosen to violently, callously take her life. I'll find a way to move on, if there is one. I just need to know for sure.

Surely, my therapist can recommend a reputable grief counselor who can help me work through the tangle of my life. I'm halfway to booking an appointment when my fingers brush against something polished and cool.

Metal and glass.

Her phone.

Oh my fucking God, it's her phone.

An agonized, ugly sound tears from my chest, and I wrap my fingers around it like someone in this empty room will steal it from me. Pulling it out, I can hardly see the screen because of the blur from moisture pooling in my eyes. Staring at it doesn't make it disappear. I can't believe it's here, but I can feel its reassuring weight in my palm. I'd recognize its pale pink vegan leather case anywhere. Elizabeth had said she checked everywhere for the phone, but neither of us had used this hiding place in nearly a decade—since we were kids—so I'm not surprised she didn't think of it. By the time I remembered, she wouldn't talk about Mom at all, let alone consider looking for it with me.

It's dead, of course, but I try the power button anyway. As much as I want to dive into it, I know I'm pressing my luck each second I linger. Stowing it away in my purse and connecting it to the power bank, I recover the panel and replace the window seat. There's a pleasant numbness suffusing my system now. Maybe I'm dissociating. It's incredible after such a long time spent hyperaware of absolutely everything.

Phone retrieved, I force myself to turn my thoughts to how to get out of the party without drawing any further attention. Once I get to the stairs, I'll ensure there isn't anyone around, like I didn't break into one of the rooms and steal something. I'm so close to finally having the answers I'm looking for, I can practically taste it.

Despite the urgency growing within me, I give the room one last prolonged study, remembering how much time I spent here with my mother. I think of her sitting with us in her lap in the window seat, reading Tuck Everlasting or The Bridge to Terabithia, and my nose stings. I'm so lost in the memories, I don't recognize the sounds on the other side of the door until it's almost too late.

There's a scuffle and a scrape, and the doorknob turns.

# CHAPTER THREE

If someone were to find me here, I could put on an act. Pretend to be drunk. Say I got lost, but all it would take would be for them to remove my mask for people to ask questions. Fear of being found out propels me across the room and into a closet stuffed with more pool cues, linens, unlabeled boxes, and mostly empty shelves. I barely make it inside with the door closed behind me when someone flings the door to the room open so hard it crashes against the wall.

"Stop fighting," says a deep, familiar voice I can't place at first, followed by the thud of something heavy and solid against the floor. The boards beneath my spiked heels quake, and I back myself into the closet, but the shelves stop my movement with a rattle of protest.

and I startle, my chest squeezing. There's nowhere to go. "Close the door," the voice orders.

Squeezing into myself is pointless, but I try to make my body as small as possible. Not that they know I'm listening to whatever confrontation is going on just a few feet away from me.

The door slams, yanking a yelp free I smother with my hand. My knees threaten to collapse beneath me, so I lock them in place and grip the shelf behind me with my free hand. A relentless drum beats in my ears, and I force myself to suck in humid breaths of air so I don't pass out and give myself away.

"Now that we have some privacy," the familiar voice continues, "do you want to tell me again what it is you're demanding? Because I'm afraid I didn't hear you clearly downstairs. So loud, you know?"

I should have left when I had the chance. If I hadn't let nostalgia grip me by the throat, I could have been gone by now, safe in an Uber back to my house. Instead, I'm stuck in this closet, listening to whatever the hell this confrontation is, and close to wetting myself from fear. My phone buzzes in my clutch with Yasmine's next 30-minute check-in text, but I don't dare fish it out, afraid the light will somehow give away my presence.

The shadows of their bodies shift in the space underneath the door. I swallow back a whimper as the door rattles. If I had to guess, whoever is speaking just threw someone against it. My stomach sinks into my ass. Whatever is going on doesn't feel benign.

"This is a misunderstanding," says a second voice, sounding so close he must be the one pressed against the door. Pinned against the door? "C'mon. We can talk about this."

"I'm afraid there won't be any more talking. This isn't the way we like to do business. We agreed upon a price, and unfortunately, renegotiations are unacceptable."

"Fine—that's f-fine. I accept our original terms. C'mon, O'Connor. Let's be reasonable. You can't do anything to me. I'm a cop. People will look for me if you touch one hair on my head. So let's stop now before you do something you'll regret."

The expensive champagne from earlier roils in my stomach, and I'm momentarily concerned for my glittering Louboutins. He can't mean O'Connor. I must have misheard. Not Aiden O'Connor. I try to become one with the shelves behind me, praying they'll magically turn into a portal and I can escape to a beach somewhere. I've always wanted to go to the Maldives. But no matter how much I try, they don't budge and allow me to disappear inside them.

For a second, I'm thrown back to when I'd been caught in his line of sight, and I must admit, I could very much see him as the type to terrify anyone, even a police officer.

Fucking fabulous.

I can only hope they'll take this little meeting somewhere else.

"I've been very reasonable about our arrangement, Dufresne, until you tried to ask for more money for your services. Then threatened my well-being. Frankly, I don't take kindly to some fuckin' arsehole trying to think they can play games with me. Especially not a dirty cop."

Well, so much for that hope.

Dread sews a lead weight lining into my stomach. All I can do is keep quiet so I don't have that terrible, menacing voice directed at me next.

"Stop wastin' your time on this piece of shite. He's not worth it." I don't recognize the third voice, but its callous disinterest in the goings-on tells me I need to stay as far away from whoever it is as possible. Only another monster could be bored by the threatening undertone in Aiden's voice.

I expect O'Connor to help the man he's insulting back to his feet. To smooth everything over and get back to the party. I don't fully understand what the guy—Dufresne—did to piss him off, and I don't want to be around to figure it out. The less I know of all of this, the better.

But I don't get to live in that dream world because in the next heartbeat, three things happen in rapid succession.

There's a click. Dufresne jolts and shouts, "No! Don't! I'll tell everyone—" but it's clipped off by a whoosh of air and a dull, wet-sounding thump.

Did he...?

No. I shake my head, my hand pressing so hard over my mouth I know I'll have bruises in the shape of my fingertips if I keep it up.

The bored voice returns. "Damn rude of him to blackmail you at a charity gala. Americans." He snorts, then comes another thud, and the body—Dufresne— jerks against the door. I shake uncontrollably. "He couldn't have waited until Monday, could he? Now I have to miss the rest of the fun to clean up this mess. I almost wish he were alive so I could kill him for the cheek."

"You'll survive. Hide him somewhere. I'll block the back elevator from the waitstaff, and we'll take care of the body tomorrow. Get one of the boys if you need help. I have to get back down to the party before I'm missed."

Of all the terrible scenarios I'd imagined could take place tonight, this had not been one of them.

I'd painted the worst picture of Aiden O'Connor since he bought my family's house. A ruthless, greedy billionaire who takes what he wants and doesn't give a damn about anything else. But all of my silly caricatures pale compared to reality.

Because Aiden O'Connor isn't only a cold-hearted, arrogant asshole.

He's a killer.

"You owe me for this," the other voice says. "Shall I just add it to your tab?"

Whatever Aiden says in response is drowned out by the sound of grunting and scraping as the other man hefts the body up and heaves it out of the door.

I hold my breath until I hear the door click behind them, and then I give myself sixty seconds to straight-up fucking panic. I didn't really hear billionaire Aiden O'Connor kill someone in cold blood right next to me, did I? This doesn't happen in real life.

Yet...

I know what I heard.

Once the sixty seconds are over, despite the ringing in my ears, despite how my fingertips have no sensation whatsoever and are shaking uncontrollably, I breathe deeply through my nose and out through my mouth. It's even more imperative than ever that I get the fuck out of here as soon as possible.

My phone buzzes again, jolting me to life, and I resolve to text Yasmine as soon as I'm safe. If I ever get out of this hellhole, that is.

Part of me wants to freeze, to stay in this closet forever, but my mom's phone propels me to crack open the door. The room is empty. There's no sign anyone else was here aside from a few drops on the floor that I ignore for the sake of my sanity.

With one last long exhalation, I cross the room to the door, one step closer to sweet freedom. Getting out of this hellhole can't happen any quicker. My trembling fingers twist the knob and pull it open. The scream that's been building in my chest for the past quarter hour rips out of my lungs when I find Aiden O'Connor waiting on the other side of the door, almost like he's not surprised to find me here—in this room. It takes me momentarily off guard, my brows knitting together.

"I thought I heard something. I should have known it was a lost little girl wandering where she shouldn't be," he says, and I loosen for a moment. If he'd known my name, he would have called me out. He slaps a hand over my mouth before I can unleash another scream or call for help. "No, no. None of that. You're not going anywhere."

He shoves me back into the room with his free hand, guiding my waist. I trip on my godforsaken towering heels and we both go crashing to the floor. His hand muffles my yelp of pain, and my body explodes into starbursts of agony. My elbows, my head, my ass.

Aiden's weight—200 plus pounds of pure lean

muscle—crashes down on me a second later with a muffled *umph* from him, squeezing what little air remains in my lungs. Tears smart at the backs of my eyes as I struggle to show no weakness.

"Christ," Aiden wheezes as he gingerly gets to his hands and knees, finally removing his hand from my face to squeeze at his crotch. It doesn't matter. There isn't enough air left in me to yell.

If I could speak, I'd tell him I'd do worse than crush his balls. Thankfully, I've retained enough of my common sense to keep my smart fucking mouth closed. I don't need to get in any more trouble than I already am.

"Fan-fucking-tastic," he hisses between pants, his knuckles turning white as he grips his muscular thighs. "Did Cian send you here to render me infertile? Fuck!"

As I sputter and cough to draw breath back into my lungs, I glare at him, which only seems to irritate him further, his frown deepening. I fist my hands over my stomach because gouging his eyes out with my new French coffin acrylics will not do me any good. The oxygen deprivation must be making me go insane.

"Want to tell me what you're doing in here? I know for a fact this door was locked."

No answer I give this man will appease him. There won't be any arguing my way out of this debacle. Even if I could come up with the perfect explanation, I know that witnessing him execute a police officer means I'm as good as dead. I can only hope to keep him talking long enough to figure out a way to escape. The ice in my veins chills me from the inside out, and I shiver under his penetrating gaze.

"It wasn't locked when I found it. I was trying to find the bathroom," I choke out, my voice croaky and hoarse.

"The bathroom," he repeats drolly. "And you couldn't find it downstairs?"

"They were full, and it's a big house. I got lost."

"Lost."

"That's right."

"How unfortunate for you," he says.

My stomach drops, but I say, "You can say that again. Do you think you could let me up now?"

Wordlessly, he pushes to his feet, and I do the same, wincing as my aching muscles protest. My thoughts whirl like a spun-out tire. I just need one opportunity to bargain my way out of here. With one chance to escape, I'll commit myself to earning a new world sprinting record. No way have I come this close to finding out what happened to my mother just for me to die before I finish what I've started.

Before he can say something else, the door wheezes open and his friend from earlier, the one with messy dark brown curls, strides in, a little out of breath.

Catching sight of us, he pauses. His eyes widen, then crinkle with amusement.

His gaze darts to Aiden, and he lifts a brow.

"Don't say a fuckin' word," Aiden spits, his accent rough and thicker than before. "Did you handle it?"

"Yes." He tips his head in my direction as he circles Aiden and me. I'm reminded of a hyena by his mad smile and predatory perusal. I'm torn between keeping an eye on him and noting he's left the path between me and the door wide open. "Do you also need me to handle... this?"

A sinking feeling tells me I don't want to know what he means by handle it.

Aiden's attention trails along my skin as though he's touching me instead of merely looking. I'd almost prefer the other guy to kill me than to have Aiden studying me so closely.

"No, I don't think so. Why don't you go downstairs and keep our guests distracted? I'll be down shortly."

Without giving them a warning, I dart for the door, my heels clicking a frantic staccato against the wood floor, but I don't get anywhere close to sweet salvation. Instead, Aiden wraps an arm around my waist and spins me around, putting his body between me and my escape.

"The absolute cheek," the other guy says, delighted. "You sure you don't want help?"

"I'm sure," Aiden says, his mouth so close to my ear I can feel his warm breath on my neck.

His friend hesitates. The mad humor left his eyes for a moment. "Don't you think—"

"I said, I'm sure. I'll be down shortly." This time, Aiden's tone brooks no argument. Even I would hesitate to defy him.

"You get to have all the fun," his friend huffs before closing the door behind him and leaving me and Aiden alone again.

Fuck.

Maybe I would have been better off with the crazy one.

With his body between me and the door, he releases me, and I spin around, not wanting to have my back to him a moment longer than necessary. His face is carefully blank of emotion, but he doesn't quite dull the rabid curiosity in his expression. It's so intense, I take a step back to dull its potency.

"I swear I won't say anything. Let me go, and you'll never see me again."

It kills something in me to say that, considering how hard I'm willing to fight and the lengths I'm willing to go to find justice for my mother. I mean, the guy just killed someone, but if he really was a corrupt police officer, then I have no sympathy for him. And I won't be able to help anyone if I'm dead.

"I'm afraid I can't let that happen," Aiden answers.

"Then what—what do you want from me?"

"I want you to tell me the real reason you were in this room and what you were doing at the party. I know everyone on my guest list, and you weren't on it."

I lift my chin. "Like hell I'm going to tell you anything. You'll probably kill me like you did that cop anyway."

His head tilts. "Yes, there's that. But I don't normally kill unarmed women. Tell me what you're doing here, and I'll consider letting you go."

"What if we flip a coin?" I blurt before he can propose something much, much more horrific.

He stills, and I hadn't even realized he was drawing closer. "A coin, really?"

"That's right. You run casinos, right? You like games of chance. What if we flip a coin or something? Heads, you let me go without a word, and I promise to keep my mouth shut. Tails, I stay and..." My voice trails off because he's looking at me like a cat would a butterfly it's about to pounce on. I swallow hard.

"Tails, you stay and... what? Please continue. I'll admit I'm intrigued."

I gulp. Intrigued is the last thing I want him to be, but it's my only choice.

"Tails, I stay and keep you company for the rest of the event."

Another shiver wracks me under his weighted scrutiny. "And what makes you think I need your company? Dozens of women downstairs would come the second I snapped my fingers."

Licking my lips, I note the way his attention drops to my mouth. "Because if you wanted to get rid of me, you would have already." He steps closer. I almost keep babbling, but I bite my tongue and wait for his response.

He'd been moving closer again, and now he's only a breath away. The backs of his fingers skim my jaw. "Fine. But I prefer dice. Even, you stay. You'll be mine to do with as I please until morning, and you'll tell me what you're doing here. Odd, you're free to go, no questions asked. Deal?"

Aiden draws a pair of dice from his pocket and shifts them over and over in his palm, the sound of them clicking together the only noise in the room until I say in a tremulous voice, "Deal."

# CHAPTER FOUR

Aiden moves, and I freeze until he passes by me toward the pool table. Releasing a breath, I push a hand through my hair, wishing I could take off the mask and wipe away the moisture underneath. I follow him at a much slower pace and nearly jump out of my skin when my phone starts frantically buzzing in my clutch, which I still miraculously have on my shoulder.

He twists, lifting one brow, and rests a hip on the side of the pool table. "Boyfriend?"

"Would you care?"

"No."

I roll my eyes. "Friend. Checking on me." I take my phone out and wave it around. "She'll keep texting if I don't answer her."

Crossing his arms, he says, "Then answer her. Tell

her you're having a grand old time, and you'll see her in the morning. But if you share anything about what happened tonight, I'm afraid the result won't be nice for either of you."

Like he had to reiterate that.

My mother's phone is exactly where I left it, still charging, if it's even still working. I secure it in a zippered pocket for extra safekeeping, and then I dig around for mine and fish it out.

There are several messages from Yasmine. Of course there are.

> Yasmine: Should I pick out an urn in case Aiden finds out what you're up to and someone goes all stalker/bodyguard on your ass?

Five minutes later.

> Yasmine: Haha, very funny. I'm dead. Answer now. I haven't had much sleep after the last few shifts. I'm already this close to crashing the fuck out. I knew I should have gone with you.

A minute after that.

> Yasmine: Really not funny tho, Ri. Check in before I lose my mind and send Reggie over there.

Followed by more of the same at one-minute intervals. It's been nearly twenty minutes since my last check-in. No wonder she's panicking. And Yasmine is usually so unruffled. It's why she's going into emergency medicine.

My fingers fly over the keyboard before she can make good on her promise.

> Me: Shit, I'm sorry. Got cornered by some drunk people on my way out and couldn't get free until now. I'm fine, I promise. I found the phone. You get some sleep. I'm waiting for my Uber, and I'll check in first thing in the morning.

I hope.

No matter what happens, I don't want her to worry.

> Yasmine: Who was your first crush?

> Me: You're joking.

> Yasmine: Answer the question, sicko, or I'm calling the cops. If you're really Catriona, then you'll know the answer.

I nearly laugh. It comes out as a choked snort. Christ. This is a literal nightmare. But goddamn, I love her with my whole heart.

Me: I hate you. Kovu from The Lion King II, you bitch.

Yasmine: You love me. Fine. I'll text you in the morning. Love your face. Glad you aren't dead.

Me: I do love you. I owe you double margs.

Yasmine: Damn right you do.

I love her so fucking much. If I make it out of this, I'll give her all the spicy margaritas she wants.

I lock my phone and stow it back in my clutch, realizing Aiden is still fixed on me like I'm a puzzle he's desperate to solve. Could he have figured out who I am? Does he recognize me from the countless news stories and social media posts with the photos of my perfect family? Oh God, I hope not.

"Alright, I told her I'm about to leave. She thinks I'm waiting on an Uber, and she's going to sleep. Please don't... go after her or something. She's completely innocent in all this." I'd die if something happened to her. Yasmine is the only person who believes me. Not even Reggie wanted to get involved in my suspicions, and he's known me since I was a baby.

Aiden's head tilts, reminding me of a cat. His

muscular arms cross over his chest. "As long as you keep your word, I'll keep mine. I won't hurt her."

"Fine," I say. "Are we going to keep talking all night, or are you going to roll the dice?"

He gives me a long, hard look and then raises his hand to my mouth, the cream-colored dice in his palm. "For luck," he says and lifts his hand higher.

When I press my lips together in answer, his mouth quirks in an oh-well gesture, like this is all a game to him.

And maybe it is.

Perhaps he wants to play with his food before eating it.

Aiden tips his hand, and the dice tumble out of it and onto the blood-red felt of the pool table. I jerk involuntarily like I'm going to grab for them to stop this farce before I'm trapped with him for the night, but he takes my arms in his and moves so quickly, I'm pinned between his body and the pool table before I can do anything. We both watch as the dice tumble and tumble and tumble until they crash into the side of the pool table and finally, finally stop. We both jerk as the number is revealed.

Snake eyes.

Two.

Probability of rolling a two? Less than 3 percent.

Less than three fucking percent.

Should I let it get to me that snake eyes are bad luck? My stomach hollows out as I consider exactly what he could have in mind for me for the rest of the night. I didn't put any stipulations on what he could and couldn't do. What does 'do with as I please' even mean to a man like Aiden O'Connor?

I dread finding out.

I'd gambled for my freedom… and lost.

"How should I have you first, pet?" he asks, his mouth unnervingly close to my ear, voice rumbling and dangerous—I'm pinned and helpless. "On your knees? Or bent over this table so I can see if you're worth the trouble?"

Shudders wrack my body as I lock my knees to stay upright. Well, I guess that answers the question of what he has in mind for me. None of it good.

"Do you think that's going to scare me?" I ask with more bravery than I feel. I'm giving up trying to interpret my emotions at this point. The one thing I do know is I can't let him see any weakness. "Because it doesn't."

Instead of pissing him off, his lips hover at my neck, and he's so close they tickle my skin as they draw into a smirk. "Alright, pet, whatever you say."

"Stop calling me that."

"Then tell me your name now and I'll call you that instead."

That's not happening.

A shiver threatens, but I turn to stone to fight it off. Chills race down my arms and tighten my nipples instead. Fantastic. "Fine," I grit out. "Call me whatever you like as long as you tell me what you want from me."

"Whatever I like?" he croons and backs off enough that I'm able to turn around in his arms. Strains of music from the party fill the momentary silence. He's close, far, far too close. But the only way to get by him would involve rubbing my body against his, and I don't plan on giving him the satisfaction. "We need to go back down to my guests. I have an alibi to establish. What better way to do that than with a beautiful woman at my side?"

A sick, greasy feeling rolls through my stomach. "You're disgusting."

His smile is a predatory carving on his beautiful face. "A fact I'll prove to you before the night is over. You should have thought of that before you gambled with me."

I knew he'd accept my offer. I just never thought I'd lose. Stupid. Playing games with men like Aiden is foolish, and I know better. "Couldn't you just kill me and save yourself the trouble?"

"Do you think they'd believe you? How are you going to prove what you saw when there won't even be a body?"

"Then why would you need an alibi?"

"I like to cover all my bases." He tries to brush the

hair away from my face, and I jerk away. He *tsks*, then says, "We'll need to work on this. Like the pretty pet you are, you need rules." When my only answer is a glare, he smiles. "Improving already."

"Just tell me the rules so we can get this over with."

"You're to stay by my side at all times. No wandering off and getting yourself into more trouble."

"I won't—"

"Like you've already done once tonight," he adds with a pointed look.

"Fine."

"No excessive drinking."

"Whatever you say." The champagne I had earlier is already giving me a headache. When I make it through tonight, I'm going to spend the rest of my life devoting myself to being boring. Focus on finishing law school. A veritable saint.

"And no talking to anyone but me."

"What the hell do you even want me around for if I'm supposed to be a statue by your side all night?"

He brings his thumb to my jaw for the second time and finally gives me the answer I demand. "Because I want to ensure you understand what will happen if you say one word about what you saw tonight or ever try to set foot near this place again."

Fear clenches my gut like a fist. "You said you weren't going to hurt me," I whisper.

"Oh, pet, by the time I'm done with you, you're going to wish I'd hurt you."

His featherlight touch dances around the shell of my ear. It takes every ounce of self-control I possess to keep from recoiling. It's too soft, a whisper of sensation. Barely anything at all. And I already know he's capable of far, far worse, but it's so gentle, it reminds me of how sweet a man can be. How attentive. How easy it could be to believe he wouldn't hurt me.

Shoving at his arm, I try to put some distance between us, but his hand comes back, lightning fast, and he's pressed so close against me, I can feel each of his breaths. His hand clamps on my jaw, immovable when it had been featherlight only seconds ago.

"Last rule. You let me touch you when I want to, however I want to. Do you understand?"

"That you're an asshole? Yeah, I think I got that."

"If you break any of my rules, what happened to that cop is going to be the least of your worries."

I have no doubt about that, so I zip my lips and promise him with murder in my eyes that there'll be retribution. It only makes him grin, and I have to wonder how the hell I got myself in this situation. Aiden gestures for me to go first, and I stride to the door like I didn't just make a deal with the devil.

The party is going full swing downstairs, completely unaware of the monster haunting my footsteps. Champagne and finger food flow freely, carted by smiling faces under black masks. Witchery is in the air, the kind only a New Orleans night can conjure. Money exchanges hands without a second thought among the craps and blackjack tables, punctuated by the drunken cheers of partygoers who've had more than their fair share by this point. We maneuver through the crowd until we find an empty table.

I drink in the sights as one well-wisher after another assails Aiden. If they know about my mother or what happened to her in this house, no one says anything. Do they even care? Aiden places a glass of water in front of me. Seizing it, I gulp down its contents, eager for the distraction, and let my thoughts drift to memories of the last time I was in this garden. It had been for my mother's 45th birthday party a few weeks before her death. Afterward, my father surprised her with a trip to South America as a present and let my sister and me go with her. It wasn't like him to be so generous, especially not with election season approaching. I was surprised by his generosity, but grateful for the time we spent together. For the first time, Elizabeth and I got to spend time with our mother without his career interfering. Little did we know it would be one of the last times we'd see her. She didn't make it to another birthday.

By the time I come back to myself, Aiden's engrossed in conversation with men I recognize vaguely from somewhere. He's arranged me at his side and slightly in a corner, where I'm mostly obscured from view of the party. He keeps me in place with one arm around my waist, loosely holding my hip, his fingers twisting into the fabric of my skirt. I shift on my feet, draining my glass of water dry so I keep from slapping his hand away.

"... let me into your little club, eh, O'Connor? How much will it cost me?"

"More than you can afford, Crawley," jeers another of the men at the table. The man, I think his name or his last name must be Hudson, because he'd practically stuck his hand in Aiden's face and said Hudson like it was supposed to mean something. Such a pretentious fucking name. Fits him perfectly.

Both men are pathetically rich in a way that has absolved them of most of life's responsibilities. I'd know, because until my mother's death, I'd been well on my way to becoming one of them. Privileged. Arrogant. Certain of my place in life and totally aware of the length and breadth of my influence.

All it would take is one moment in time for that carefully constructed world to come crashing down around them. Life's funny that way. Sort of like how I ended up here when I'd intended to run in and out without ever drawing any attention to myself.

Aiden's gaze shifting my way is the only thing that

keeps me from rolling my eyes at this entire scenario. Definitely not on the list of Aiden-approved behavior. Judging by the mocking laughter dancing in his eyes, he's enjoying my pain and seeming lack of self-control.

What does he get out of this anyway? It has to be some kind of twisted game. A punishment for whatever reason he's cooked up inside his fucked-up brain about why I'm here. Guaranteed, he's so far off the mark it's comical.

With our eyes locked, the argument between the two men fades into the background, and my annoyance at their conversation ebbs momentarily. He's got this way of looking at me that gets under my skin. It makes me want to peel it off so I can remove every piece of evidence that he gets to me. Because, goddammit, he does. Burrows deep. Like a splinter.

You'd have to be cold and dead not to be affected by a man like Aiden O'Connor. Even if he's a cold-blooded killer. Or maybe I've gone crazy enough over the past several months that his shooting someone is the least of my worries.

"I can afford it," the first man objects. "You're the one dropping a small fortune at Caesars every weekend. Bet your wife loves that."

"What she doesn't know won't hurt her."

Both men angle their bodies away from Aiden and toward me at my snort. Aiden's hand tightens on my hip in warning, and the sound chokes off in the back of my throat. Well, it didn't take me long to break those rules after all.

"Something funny, sweetheart?" Crawley—or is it Hudson?—asks. Honestly, they both look alike, so it's hard to tell them apart.

They preen as Aiden finally seems to pay them a lick of notice. He'd mostly been reclining in his chair opposite the two, enjoying knowing that it made me so uncomfortable. But his attention swings in their direction now that they've noticed me, and their smug laughter cuts off. He says nothing, so Crawley/Hudson grows more confident, emboldened by Aiden's regard.

"Yeah," the other says. "Something funny?"

I open my mouth to respond, then sense Aiden's presence like a shadow out of the corner of my eye and think better of it. I'm not the type of woman to hold my tongue, but I bite back the retort that threatens to leap free, no matter how much I want to tear into them.

"Why don't you stop by my office on Monday, Hudson?" Aiden says, and it's like they completely forget me. "We'll talk, and I'll see what I can do."

With them distracted, Aiden tugs me from my standing position at his side into his lap. Clutching his imposing shoulders is the only way I can keep myself from flying off his lap to the other side. His hands settle around my waist, so broad they nearly span the width of my hips.

"I was perfectly fine standing," I mutter as he lifts his hand to catch the eye of a passing server. He gestures for what he wants, and the server nods so fast, I'm afraid her head may fall off.

"And now I'm ready for you to sit," he says, voice low and so close to my ear it creates a sense of intimacy I'd rather do without.

"Why?"

"Because it's what I want."

"And you're used to getting what you want," I surmise. I'm not surprised. Based on the greeting he got when he walked into the party earlier, it's easy to imagine he gets whatever he wants whenever he wants it.

"You would think that," he says, and I shift slightly, hoping to put some space between his body and mine, but his arms tighten around me. "Stop wiggling."

"I can't help it. I can sit in my own chair, you know."

"If I wanted you to sit somewhere else, I would have put you there."

"Are you always this controlling, or am I just lucky?"

"Your smart mouth is going to get you in trouble," he says, moving his mouth closer to my ear, not missing when the sensation makes me suck in a sharp breath.

"Then again, you did break into my game room, so maybe you were looking for trouble."

"How did you know I broke in?"

"Just assume I know everything."

"I'm sure you'd like to think that, wouldn't you?"

Aiden shifts my body until my ass settles firmly in his lap, my back against the broad expanse of his chest. He wraps his muscular arms around me until my senses are filled with him. From his heat to his strength to his scent—rainstorms and wood-smoke.

Hudson and Crawley focus intently on the game, already forgotten by Aiden, but I become more intensely aware of their presence as Aiden slides his big palms along my thighs, reaching the end of my too-short dress all too soon. My hand flies out to cover his to stop their upward trajectory. Tingles pepper along my skin from where it comes into contact with his devilish touch. They glide up my nerve endings and sizzle through my blood. Is it because of my fear and aware-ness of all the people around us that I am hyper-focused on the way his palms are rougher than I expect?

His psychotic chuckle rumbles against my back. "You want to break two of those rules so quickly, pet?" His thumbs swipe up the sensitive flesh of my inner thigh, causing the tingles to multiply. "So eager for a punishment, aren't you?"

"Eager to get this over with so I can get the fuck out

of here, maybe," I mutter, but it comes out too breathless to lend my denial any credence. His hands resist mine, tugging them along for the ride as they trawl indecently high up my thighs.

No one is paying us any mind. By now, the crowd has taken full advantage of the open bar, and most of the media who'd been interviewing at the start of the event have been escorted off the premises. We could be alone for all the concern the people around direct to us.

"Is that what you think?" The words are pressed from his lips to my throat. His mask, a chilling contrast where it meets my skin.

"Ye-yes."

As much as I try to ignore the sensation, it's impossible.

"That's too bad. I told you there were rules when you rolled those dice. You keep your mouth shut, and you let me do whatever I want, whenever I want. I think it's time you learned what that means."

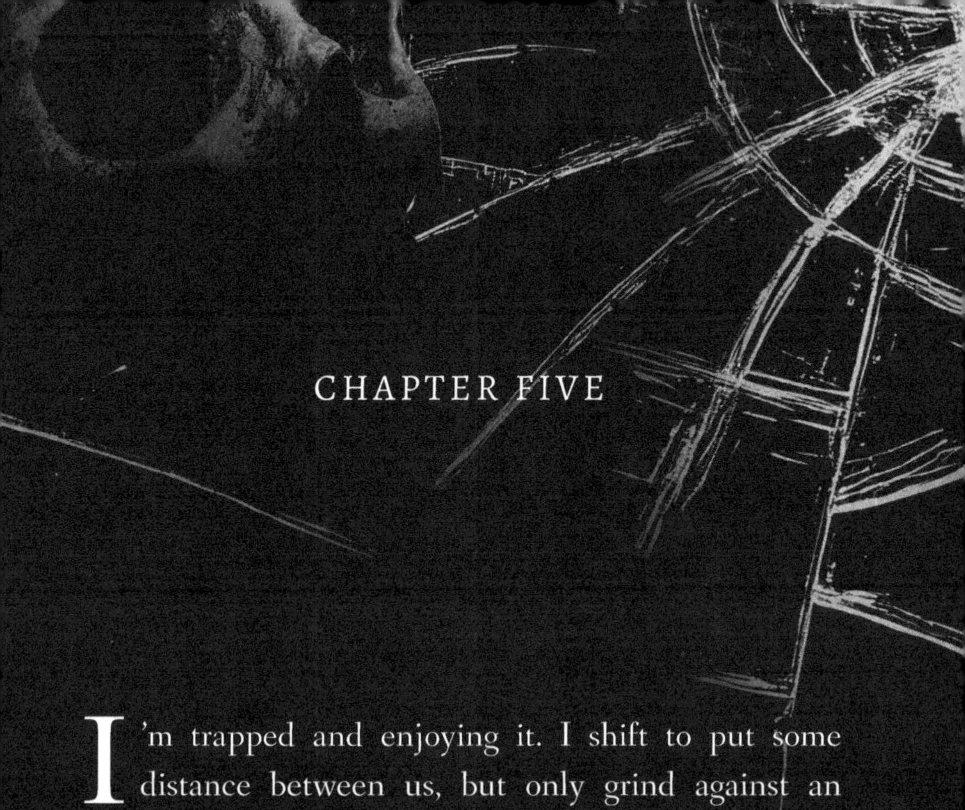

# CHAPTER FIVE

I'm trapped and enjoying it. I shift to put some distance between us, but only grind against an impressive erection.

Sensing the tension stitching into my muscles, he says, "Relax. If I wanted anyone to know what I was doing to you, they would. Luckily for you, I prefer to keep my business to myself."

We fight over control of the territory of my upper thighs despite his warning, and he quickly overpowers me by taking both of my hands in one of his. His free hand slips beneath the hem of my dress and slides upward between my legs without hesitation. I suck in a breath, and it sounds like a gunshot in my head, but the band playing on the stage near the back of the property and the buzz of conversation and shouts from the dealers drown it out.

Struggling against him quickly proves to be a fruitless endeavor. Those rough, capable hands keep me well and truly trapped against his firm body as his fingers trace over the whisper of my minuscule panties. I should have fucking worn slacks, but that thought melts away as horror drains it out. My struggles increase, despite the futility, because I can't let him know, can't let him discover...

"Oh, pet, is this all for me?" he croons in my ear, his brogue thick with pleasure.

I freeze, mentally flying away to somewhere, anywhere, that isn't here. Humiliation flames hot, though, keeping me too present to ignore as Aiden strokes the tip of one finger over the damp lace coating my pussy. He strokes down the outside of my underwear, pressing against the material to the point of obscenity. His moan of satisfaction sends me crashing back to reality.

Cheeks aflame, I try to turn away to get back to that floaty place where this doesn't exist, but his fingers bite into my skin, keeping me firmly present and aware of what he's doing to me. "You don't get to hide away. You want to know what your punishment is for letting those men hear you? You get to come."

My first thought is to snort again, until I realize

that's what got me into this mess, and I resist. It doesn't sound like much of a punishment. Then, his finger does another lingering pass over my underwear. "Don't. Not here. You don't have to do this. I'll be quiet, I promise."

Anyone could see us.

It could be splashed all over the news.

How am I more worried about this than he is? He touches me with abandon, completely unconcerned—or completely consumed by the thought of it — that everyone else here ceases to exist for him. We exist in a bubble where no one else can intrude. His singular focus is on me, and I quiver with terror, shame, and something too close to excitement to examine.

The things I'm learning about myself tonight will take a therapist a lifetime to unravel.

"I don't want your promises. You're already going to do whatever I want. Aren't you?" Before I can answer, he's inside me and sparks dance behind my closed eyelids.

The party continues around me as though Aiden isn't finger-fucking me in the middle of it. Instead of struggling more, I grip his wrists, needing an anchor so I don't simply fly away. A moan bubbles up in my throat, and I choke on it until I can breathe properly. It may be my imagination, but I swear the wet glide of his fingers thrusting in and out of me can be heard by everyone at the party.

"Aiden, we could—someone could see," I sob.

"They could," he admits, surprising the protests from my lips. "I could fuck you in front of them and you'd have to let me. But what you want tonight doesn't matter. All that matters is that you understand what will happen if you ever come back."

"I won't, I won't, I swear," I pant.

His mouth presses to my ear again, and he must have noticed how it makes every part of me clench. He says, "I don't believe you. I told you I wouldn't hurt you, but I'm going to spend the rest of the night making you break over and over for me. When I'm done with you, I'll bet every cent in my bank account you'll wish I had."

Panic spirals inside me as the party continues and Aiden's fingers drive me higher and higher into madness. I fist the material of my dress, realizing belatedly he'd released his grip on me. Then his thumb comes into play, stroking across the sensitive, throbbing mess of my clit with firm, even pressure. Jolting back against him makes him bite my earlobe in warning.

"I don't want you to make a sound. Drawing attention to yourself will only make your punishment worse. I'll make you come so many times you'll beg me to stop. Is that what you want? Why do you keep grinding your pussy into my hand? Do you want everyone to see what a good little slut you're being for me?"

I don't answer. I can't. My jaw is physically incapable of letting words pass my lips. My teeth stay glued together, and as long as I keep my eyes closed, I can pretend this is happening to someone else. Once again, I'm outside my body, a victim to the riot of sensations, until the band kicks up their set, smashing drums and cranking up the volume to play a cover of a popular song. Footsteps gallop to the makeshift dance floor, heedless of my torment.

The increase in volume covers my yelp when Aiden removes his fingers from my pussy to give me a sharp *slap, slap* right over the top of my clit, jolting me back to him. Eyes flying open, I jerk. As soon as I focus on him, his fingers return to me, sliding through the mess of my arousal and plunging so deep inside me I've never felt more connected to another human.

His strokes are slow now, but sure. His body is granite beneath and around me, immovable and unfeeling aside from where he stokes me to life. The way he masters me is thought-melting. Rationality? Who's she?

As much as I want to fight against him, the swell of a devastating orgasm unfurls low in my belly, coaxed to life by his fingers, the thrill of getting caught, and his absolute command over my body. Our mouths hover a breath away from each other, all my protests imprisoned in my chest. For one crazed moment, all I can think about is closing the distance and kissing him.

How is he about to make me come, and I've never kissed him?

That realization is followed closely by the deep, irrefutable knowledge that there's a terrifying possibility I'd let him do a whole lot worse. Including all the filthy suggestions he planted in my brain. I'd get on my knees for him. I'd let him bend me over this table with everyone watching.

Because he's taking me in like I'm the only woman in the room. Like making me come is his sole mission in life. And being the object of his obsession is the most powerful aphrodisiac I have ever known.

I've never wanted or craved having a man speak to me the way Aiden has, but maybe I like it because it's him saying it. Because he's powerful. Dangerous. And all of that lethal focus is captivated by me. Those silver eyes gleam in the low outdoor lighting, rapt. By my gasps and twitches. My rolling hips. His fist clamps on my thigh to yank me wider, and I shudder, feeling surrounded by him, consumed by him.

"You don't want to like it, but you do, don't you?" he murmurs, his accent thick and almost unintelligible, rough with gravel and as breathless as I feel. "Do you think you've learned your lesson about what happens to little girls who wander where they're not supposed to? Do you think I should take pity on you and let you go?"

I keen an inaudible sound into the place between his

head and shoulder where I bury my face. "Yes" is the word that tumbles out unbidden.

At the sound of my voice, Aiden adds a third finger, stuffing me so full that I can barely breathe. "You should know better than to think I'll show you any sort of mercy. I have you for the rest of the night, and this is only the beginning. You're going to be my perfect little slut and come all over my fingers, or make sure everyone can see what a bad girl you are for me. Come for me now, slut, or I'll—"

I don't get to hear what sick, depraved consequence he's going to dream up for me next, because my body reacts like it belongs to him, and I come, muscles contracting around his fingers, clamping down so hard he can barely move them inside me. It takes a great deal of his considerable strength to continue driving his fingers inside as the hot, thick wave of my orgasm fights against him. The powerful bunching of his muscles, the groan of his satisfaction, and the threat of his determination drag out its intensity, leaving me wrung out and deliciously spent in his lap.

Whatever he says next in the aftermath is lost in the ringing of my ears, and the only remaining sensation is the hollowness inside me when he removes his fingers. I have enough awareness to take it in as he licks each one clean like he's tasting a Michelin-starred dessert. He moves me as if I weigh nothing until I'm cradled sideways against his chest. I rest there, trying to get my heart rate under control, trying to understand how thoroughly tonight has gone off the rails and what I could have done differently to prevent it.

Aiden's hand grips one of my knees, his thumb stroking back and forth, and I stare at it, wondering if he notices what he's doing. Around us, the band is in full swing, the partygoers still completely oblivious. Most of the guests writhe together on the dance floor, faces sweaty and flushed.

When I glance up to check, his eyes are already on me. I open my mouth to speak and am furious that I hesitate, causing him to grin, white teeth flashing in the shadows.

"Learning so well, aren't we? You can talk now. What is it?"

The only reason I don't tear his head off at the patronizing response is because I'm too blissed out from what was possibly the best orgasm I've ever had. "You've made your point. You don't have to do it again. I've already told you I will not say anything. If you let me go, I'll promise whatever you need to ensure I won't say a word about what I saw."

His thumb continues its soothing path back and forth across my knee. "See how sweet you are after your punishment? How do you behave? Imagine how you'll feel after a night of it? After I make you come dozens of times. By the time the sun rises, I'll have had you screaming for so long you'll be begging to tell me what you're doing here. That's when we'll be done. When I know the thought of my face will make you hesitate before coming back. I don't trust a damn word out of your mouth, but I can trust that."

Already, the tendrils of apprehension snake through my resolve, clouding my certainty and polluting my judgment. I don't want to come back here, and the night's only just started.

Then I think about my mother and the potential clues she might have left behind. Would I have come back again to see if there was something else I might have missed?

I don't need to ask myself the question twice, because despite everything that's happened, I wouldn't hesitate.

There isn't anything I wouldn't do for her.

Even if it meant putting myself in Aiden's path again.

The question comes out before I can rip it back. "What went on between you two? Why would you kill him?" Curiosity killed this foolish cat. Isn't that how I wound up in this predicament in the first place?

He takes a long beat to answer. One that's filled with the kind of scrutiny I'm coming to ascribe to being the object of his intense focus. Something I hadn't wanted to be, until now.

"You really don't have any clue who I am, do you?" He seems almost surprised. And amused? I try to put space between us to study his expression more, but his arm tightens.

"Only what I could find on the internet after you..." I nearly choke, remembering I can't give him any clue about who I am. "Announced the casino's grand opening."

"Interesting," he says, drawing out the word.

"I assume you will not answer."

"I—" he begins, and then a familiar voice drowns him out.

"I should have known you couldn't leave the little bird alone."

"I thought you left," Aiden says flatly as he lifts me to my feet, holding a hand to my hip to keep me steady as my gelatinous knees threaten to collapse beneath me. I wrap the strap of my purse over my shoulder, despite the fuzziness clouding my brain. There's no way I'm leaving this goddamn house without it, no matter what hell he puts me through.

The nameless man studies me with deep blue eyes that see too much, burn too bright. I almost want to hold my hands out in front of my face to keep him from peering too close. Letting him study my face and draw conclusions about what Aiden just did to me. Thankfully, my mask blocks him from seeing too much, and his attention swings back to Aiden. A breath stutters from my lips, my lungs screaming from holding it for so long. "It's a good thing I didn't. I thought you said you had a handle on this and didn't need any help."

Aiden merely lifts a brow. "What makes you think I don't have a handle on this, Eamon?" Before Eamon can answer, Aiden turns to me. He dips his head in a nod toward the house and leans down so only I can hear his words. "Why don't you go inside and freshen up? There's a guest bath off the kitchens, and I'll find you when I'm done." His eyes drill into mine. "I don't need to say if you do something stupid, the punishment will be far, far worse. You understand?"

I don't want to know what could be worse than what he just did, but I also don't want to find out what else he has in store for me. So I nod, keeping my face carefully blank and wobbling my way through the departing crowd, careful to be as discreet as possible. My heart rams against my chest the whole way inside, certain someone is going to stop me and rail at me for what we've just done. But no one does. Too hammered, too coked out, too depressed from losing too much money. Take your pick. Bodies filter out of the front door in droves. Most of the detritus has been cleared away, and catering staff flit around like bees, collecting what remains as I weave through them. My heels click against the marble floors, the sound echoing in my pounding ears.

A hot, prickling spot comes to life between my shoulder blades, and I know it's his eyes glued to my back. Always watching. I don't allow myself to be swept away by the crowd. Not when he's on high alert. But I'd be an idiot not to take this as an opportunity. One I may not have again.

By the time I reach the downstairs bathroom near the kitchen, my whole body quakes, both from the aftermath of what he did to me, but also from the colossal rush of adrenaline. I close the door behind me, giving him time to think I'm following his orders. I rip away my mask, needing to feel fresh air on my overheated skin, and I nearly wince at what it uncovers.

Wrecked.

Mascara smudges beneath my eyes. Red blush stains my cheeks that no amount of cool water from the faucet seems to wash away. An over-bright, manic glare in my otherwise plain brown eyes. My mother's eyes.

With one encounter, Aiden O'Connor has torn off my carefully crafted veneer. And, God help me, my body aches for more of him. More depravity. More ownership. It capitulated to him without a second thought. He'd mastered it so thoroughly that my goal of getting out of here had disappeared entirely from my mind. I'd even started feeling sympathetic toward him, and that's after I witnessed him execute someone not even an hour ago.

A healthy number of mediocre men have made me come before. It means nothing.

It doesn't.

Just because I take much longer to convince myself to at least try to escape means nothing either.

A quick check reveals that my phone is dead. I nearly throw it at the wall in frustration, but put it on the charger bank instead. If it had been working, I would have sent a text to Yasmine for backup. But just my fucking luck.

I tie my mask firmly back in place around my head and peer out of the door, stomach sinking when I note the empty halls and foyer beyond. Shit. So much for trying to blend in with the crowd. In fact, almost everyone is gone. The band. The servers. Even Aiden and his friends aren't loitering in the back garden anymore. My ears strain to receive sound, but all I hear is the relentless drum of my heartbeat. It's eerily quiet. Like a graveyard and all that's left of the party are the echoes of voices knocking around in my head, haunting me like ghosts. A chill grips my spine and doesn't let go.

There are two options. Both equally shitty. The front door is to my left, the closest option. But it's also the one he'll most likely expect. My second option is the garage, which spills out onto a busier street, making it easier to hide if I manage to escape.

Fingers fumbling, I unhook the clasps on my shoes and grip them in nerveless fingers. It's now or never. My heart skips a beat, and I press my hand to my chest to assuage the ache. This is my chance. Fuck his warnings. Fuck his threats. Fuck his deal. I'm going to get out of here before I do anything else stupid, like crawl for him or beg him to call me a slut again.

I'm running when he and his friend appear in the doorway to the kitchen, only a few feet away. The sound of a muttered curse and the rhythmic thud of his shoes striking the tile sounds behind me, but I don't dare look back.

# CHAPTER SIX

"Oh shit," Eamon says. He chuckles, and I pick up speed, because there's no way in fuck I want to be anywhere he is. I swear that guy has something fucked up in his brain. And that's saying something after what I just did with Aiden. After what I saw Aiden do.

"Do you want help now?" Eamon adds in a lifted voice, his accent ricocheting off the empty rooms.

"Fuck off," Aiden huffs—too close for comfort.

"I'll see you later then, lad," Eamon singsongs, and the slamming of a door punctuates his manic laughter. The sound chases me down the hall as surely as Aiden does.

Seriously, what the fuck is wrong with these people?

My legs and arms pump. Breath saws out of me. I

make it three-quarters of the way down the hall toward the wing of the house that contains the garage before I let myself experience a starburst of hope. Almost to freedom. I can do this. I'm going to make it. The garage door opener is on a panel next to the door. All I have to do is get there, shut the door behind me, hit the garage door button, and then roll out from underneath it. As soon as I get a good way down the street, I'll order a car to meet me several roads over.

Everything will be fine.

I can make it.

Exhilaration threads through my blood, stitching all the broken parts of me back together one by one. A part of me shattered the night my mother was murdered. In the months since, the pieces must have healed wrong. Crooked. Jagged. Because I bite back the impulse to smile. A psychologist would have a field day with this scenario, let me tell you that. I'd try to explain the first time I experienced something like joy, since my mother's violent death was at the hands of a violent psychopath, and they'd lock me up and throw away the key. I can't tell anyone about this. Maybe not even Yasmine.

Terror, sweet and biting, swells in my chest. I can't let him catch me. But at the same time...

Part of me wants him to.

It's as much fear of that knowledge as fear of him that keeps my legs going. A knife of pain threads through my ribs, and my lungs seize, but I don't stop. Something about this fear electrocutes me out of the half-dead state I've been in for the past six months. Like what we did during the party revives all the stagnant parts of me. It's addictive, this feeling. I try to shake this madness away, remind myself that he's dangerous, but a feral euphoria seeps into my skin, melting into my very soul, my DNA, rewriting everything I thought I knew about myself.

Fear has been such an integral, inescapable part of my life since she died, to the point where I thought I'd drown in it. But having Aiden chase me? It takes that fear, warps it, kinks it, until I crave it. Makes it something vital. Primal.

Twisting, I glance back to find him only a few feet away, almost within grasping distance. My nerveless feet stumble on the slick tile, and I right myself, losing precious seconds, with Aiden gaining behind me. He's so close, I swear I can feel his breath on the back of my neck, his fingers twining in the fabric of my dress. Frantic laughter bubbles free, or maybe I'm choking on the lack of oxygen reaching my brain. Despite whatever seductive alchemy of fear and exhilaration he inspires, I have to get away.

In the next second, muscular arms pluck me from the air, and my scream rends the stillness of the night before a big hand clamps over my mouth. "Did you really think you could run from me?" Aiden hisses, pressing his face to my throat, clenching me against his body.

Instinct takes over, and I claw at the arms restraining me, but he's as immovable as the ancient live oaks in the front yard. My feet pinwheel in front of me, shoes flying from my hands going God knows where, and then he's dragging me away from the garage door. Despite my cries, his hands are unforgiving against my skin, which surrenders to his bruising grip like the skin of a ripe peach.

Luck must take pity on me because our combined weight causes Aiden to stumble backward into the wall, and his grip loosens for the barest second. Using it to my advantage, I go completely dead in his arms, letting gravity carry me down through his hold, and I land heavy on my ass. Without pausing, I slap the ground, pushing to my feet, and then I'm running once again. Only this time, Aiden is much, much closer and exponentially more pissed off. His anger is almost as thrilling as the fear. His anger, unlike so much in my life, is something I understand.

"Run as fast as you can because if I catch you, I'll punish you in ways that'll make the devil blush," he calls from behind me.

I don't answer. I can't. Any oxygen my greedy lungs suck in is used for more important things than talking.

Like panicking. Trying to remain conscious. Or laughing hysterically.

Taking the next left, I reach a short hallway that includes the kitchen to my right and the pantry and garage access on the opposite wall. Relief pours into me, and I repeat my plan in cadence with each slap of my feet against the floor. Get to the garage. Brace the door behind me. Open the garage. Escape.

Behind me, Aiden gains ground, feet pounding a relentless rhythm, and I'm flooded with the exhilaration not unlike the kind I used to feel when playing hide-and-seek with Elizabeth or being chased on the playground at school when I was a kid. Except this isn't a game. I know he'll make good on his threats.

I slam into the garage door and spin to shut it behind me, but it's too late. He's too close. A panicked cry tears from my throat as Aiden collides with me before I can close it in his face. We grapple, his weight pressing in as I throw my body against the surface of the door, and it groans under the assault. Despite my efforts, he's so much stronger that I may as well not be resisting at all.

In a stroke of bad luck, the door flies open from the strain, and we stumble. Momentum carries me around until I land on top of Aiden, who grunts at the impact. Before he can trap or pin me, I'm up and sprinting. I slap at the garage door control and find a set of golf clubs on the rack nearest to me, and before I can think too much about it, I grab one and swing wildly. To my surprise, it connects with Aiden's face, and his head whips to the side.

Frozen in shock, I can only stare as Aiden slowly shifts until I can see a dark trail of blood streaming from his nose. He swipes at it with the back of his hand, staring at the smudge with an expression of curiosity.

A laugh bubbles up my throat, and I clap a hand over my mouth as it spills over. He smiles, blood on his teeth, like he's... enjoying himself?

*Fuck me.*

The garage door rattles mechanically, pulling me from my stupefaction, and I escape through the small opening before Aiden comes to his senses. Concrete scratches my knees raw, but I'm on my feet and racing down the dimly lit residential street, my soles protesting as sticks and tiny rocks assault them. A crowd bustles at the edge of the street, salvation so close I can practically feel the calming weight of relief washing through my chest.

Then I'm flying, and Aiden's arm is back around my waist, holding me tight to his body. Waves of heat slam into me, and I wrench this way and that, but it's futile. No amount of kicking, slapping, or even biting seems to deter him. He drags me kicking and screaming back down the road, his other hand has a bruising grip over my face once more.

"A valiant effort, pet. But you'll never be able to outrun me." But he doesn't sound very much like he wants me to stop. No, I'd bet he's enjoying the struggle as much as he did playing with me in the middle of the party. The evidence is undeniable. His thick, hot length presses like an iron brand into my back, sending liquid bolts of pleasure in a wet spill between my thighs.

When I don't do as he says and instead try to rip free again, he merely throws me over one broad shoulder and plants a hand on my ass, the other arm going around my thighs as I tip precariously.

"I can walk," I snarl at his back, my hands fisted in the material of his white shirt so I don't fall. My purse dangles from where it hangs on my elbow, slapping against his side, but he doesn't seem to notice. His muscles ripple with each step as he strides quickly back to the estate. "Let me down."

"Not a fuckin' chance, sweetheart. I'm going to put you somewhere you can't run from me," he says, as we reach the garage and he hauls me through.

A sense of foreboding, more terrifying than having him chase me, knots up inside my stomach. Fuck. Fuck. This is bad. Whatever punishment he's going to give me for trying to run away will be a million times worse than the one I got for drawing attention to myself in front of two of his guests.

We reach the stairs, and he takes them two at a time,

heedless of my fists beating a wild tattoo on the rippling muscles of his back. With each step up, I fight harder, but I may as well be a gnat for all it affects him. I'm not unaffected, however. The desire he'd brought to life in me hadn't diminished with my frantic dash through the house. No, running had only stoked it into a blaze.

I want to tear into him. Want to rub myself all over him. Want him to fill all the aching, empty parts of me.

"Let me go," I pant at his back, but my words are so breathless they have no substance. It doesn't even matter. He wouldn't have chased me down if he had planned to let me go before this night was over.

We reach a door, and he shoulders through it, then kicks it shut, locking it with a key he stows in his pocket. Trapped. He releases me, and I stumble to my knees, my hands slapping on the parquet floor to keep from face-planting on the wood. Without looking up, I know we're in my parents' room, which only heightens my conflicting emotions. This is absolutely the last place I want to be.

I pause there at his feet, nostrils flaring and fanta-sizing about all the ways I could hurt him. It's that or try to run again, but my whole body aches something fierce. Ass and skull from where I landed the first time, lungs from my mad dash, and various places where Aiden's fingers have branded and bruised me. But I've never felt so fucking alive. All I should feel is disgust and fear. Desperation. Disappointment.

Since I feel none of those things, I reach for the nearest hefty object—a coffee-table book on a side table—and throw it at Aiden's retreating back. It collides with him, and he stops. The way he turns, a slow revolution with the golden light coming in behind him, is menacing. Fraught. Yet I'm not scared. Or if I am, I enjoy it.

My blood thumps.

My heart sings.

But he doesn't come closer with the promised punishment. Instead, he backs away, and I ignore the swoop of my stomach. Back, back, back, until his legs hit the bed, and he lowers himself onto the foot. I push up to my knees, waiting where I fell by the door. The dark hides my eager expression. This back-and-forth game we're playing scares me almost as much as it excites me.

"Come here," he beckons.

I lift my chin, conscious of the way my dress gapes between my breasts and rides up my thighs. "No chance in hell," I say from my place on the floor. It may be across the room, but it still feels like I'm kneeling for him. "You'll have to make me."

His chuckle wraps around me like dark silk. "Make you? Oh, I don't think I'll have to make you do anything. That's why you're being such a brat, right? Because a part of you likes what I'm doing to you? Likes when I scare you. Isn't that right?"

"Fuck you."

Instead of angering him more, my hissed words only make his lips curve at one corner. "You're only digging yourself a bigger grave. Because every time you piss me off, you owe me another orgasm." His finger swipes at his nose. Is he still bleeding? "I think we're up to four now. Five?"

"Is that really supposed to scare me?" I'm glad the words come out steady, because the thought actually scares me. How many orgasms would it take for him to break me apart? See all the twisted, fucked-up things inside me? Like how many licks to the center of a lollipop. Only whatever's hiding inside me will not be something sweet.

"Does it?"

"What?"

"Does it scare you?"

"It'll take a lot more than these silly games to scare me, O'Connor," I say.

"Is that so?"

"Yeah," I punch out.

But it doesn't piss him off like I expect. His smile widens, a flash of white in the shadows. Glinting in the moonlight.

He pushes to his feet, and all my muscles tense, hands fisting at my thighs. Heart rattling in my chest. He strolls to where I'm kneeling. At his height—Jesus, is he, what, 6'4, 6'5?—he towers over me. For a moment, he considers me with glittering chips of diamond for eyes, and then in a flash, he fists a hand in my hair. One quick movement later, there's a gun pressed against my temple. The only warning is a flash of metal in a sliver of light. I don't get a good look, but I know without inspection that it's the same one he used to kill Dufresne.

Blood smears over his lips from where I hit him. It makes him look like a pagan deity. Untamable. Wild. The gun twitches, the icy edge a wicked threat that slices straight to my core. A needy sound stings my throat, spilling over my lips.

His eyes widen, then glint with satisfaction. When he speaks, his voice is low and entrancing. "Are you ready to do as you're told, like a good little pet, or do I need to scare you a bit to keep you in line?"

I could speak. Could do what I'm told. But if I'm going to spend the night with the devil, I won't make it easy on either of us. And maybe this man, this insane, ruthless man, is exactly who I need to rip me out of my brain.

Even if it's only for one night.

Amused, accepting, somehow reading my mind, he

jerks my head back, eyes roving over my face. Then he's leading me across the bedroom floor, guided by his hand in my hair like it's a leash.

And I crawl for him, just like he wanted.

# CHAPTER SEVEN

The gun bites a little deeper into my temple with every foot of progress I make across the bedroom floor. Both his fist in my hair and the gun at my head make the movements awkward, but he doesn't seem to mind how long it takes. He hovers at my side, a constant threat. Unforgiving hardwood bites into my knees, but I grind back my complaints between the flats of my teeth.

Each time I move, the gun bobs against my skull, reminding me how completely I'm at his mercy. One wrong move and my blood could be all over his hands. Like Aiden chasing me, placing my life in his hands, especially given what I witnessed him do, should terrify me. And it does. But it's also exhilarating. I'm light-headed with anticipation, wondering what he could do next.

When we finally reach the bed, there's a raw spot on my temple from the muzzle, my knees are bruised to all hell, and my panties are so soaked I can feel the wetness slicking the inside of my thighs. Hot shame heats my cheeks. It wouldn't take much investigation for him to realize how much I'm enjoying this. How much I don't want him to stop.

Aiden retakes his seat at the foot of the bed, letting the gun rest under his hand on the mattress beside his thigh. I'm kneeling in front of him, his legs on either side of me, and I don't dare move now. My whole body trembles, waiting to see what my punishment will be. Waiting? Craving? Wanting?

Fuck.

Needing.

Is that what this incessant buzzing sensation under my skin is?

Studying his face is impossible, the way the shadows fall across it. The silence is a heavy weight pressing in around me. I'm practically chewing on it, it's so thick. "What are you waiting for?" I say when I can't wait any longer. His eyes crinkle behind his blank white mask. I shiver, wishing I hated it. Wishing it were disgusting. But not knowing sends another fresh bolt of heat straight to my pussy. "Please just get it over with."

He lifts the hand not holding the gun and tips up my chin. "There it is. All you had to do was say please, so pretty for me. Was that so hard? What's next, pet? Will you cry for me? Let me taste your sweet tears?"

Heat springs up behind my eyes, making my throat sting and my voice raw when I say, "Go to hell."

His hand grips my jaw, not letting me jerk away when he leans closer. Silver eyes behind his mask gleam in the low light. "If I go anywhere, I'm taking you with me. Now lie over my lap like a good girl."

"Wh-what?" I sputter. "I thought you said orgasms were my punishment! I'm not doing—"

In the next second, his hand is around my throat, choking off my protestations. The flare of heat sitting low in my belly ignites into a small blaze. "Six. Are you greedy for that many orgasms, sweet girl? Is that why you keep fighting? Think I won't deliver? I told you that you didn't need to be a brat. I'll give you exactly what you need. I'm not like the boys you toy with. I'm a man who keeps his promises. Now lay your sweet arse over my lap. You won't like what happens if I have to tell you again." His head tilts. "Or maybe you will. Either way, I'm getting what I want. So go ahead. Test me. I. Dare. You."

Scarlet heat licks up my body from my chest to my hairline. He's going to make me do this, no matter what I say, no matter what I do. The fact shouldn't make me so desperately, insanely wet, but it does. If I sprawl over his lap, my short dress will no doubt rise to give him a full view. The evidence would be undeniable. I'm afraid he'll be able to see it, slicking the inside of my thighs. It might even soak his dress pants by the time he's done with me.

Despite my shame, the siren song of his masterful hands is too alluring to deny. One taste of him hadn't been enough. The desire he brought to life is a raging inferno inside me, and no amount of embarrassment seems to be enough to keep me from pushing to my feet. I nearly stumble, but I right myself before I fall on him and lower myself awkwardly onto his lap. With sure economical movements, his calloused hands arrange me to his liking.

I press my scalded cheek into the bedspread. The material is cool against the rawness of my skin. It's so dark, I can barely see a few feet in front of me, which heightens all my senses. His masculine scent. The sound of my rapid breathing. His body surrounds me, enveloping me. A trill of fear skates down my spine. He places a big hand on my back to still my squirming, and I stop breathing altogether.

He's got me so on edge that when his palm travels down to the back of my thigh, I jerk against him like I've been electrocuted. "Easy, pet. We're just getting start-ed," he murmurs.

With one hand resting comfortably on my back, the other glides over my ass, ghosts down the backs of my thighs, then reaches my ankles. He shifts, allowing him to reach my feet. One at a time, he pulls them up for inspection and *tsks* at the sight of their abuse. Slowly, torturously, he cleans them of debris, brushing them in confident, methodical strokes. They're tender and covered in scrapes, so each touch sends arcs of sensation shooting upward along my nerves. Too much? Too sensitive? Not enough. I can't fucking tell anymore.

When he's done with both, he arranges me back on my knees, bent over his lap, and the hand on my back moves to a warning brace across my shoulders to keep me in place. My heart stumbles as his touch nears the apex of my thighs. Like he's reading my mind, the hand bracing me increases pressure as though he knows I'm thinking about bolting. He's not wrong. The urge tightens all my muscles into knots.

"Easy," he says.

Yeah, right.

As if by magic, a light flicks on. A remote? Then, so quick it leaves me breathless, his wandering hand flips the skirt of my dress up and over my ass, baring my tiny excuse for a thong to him. Because it's little more than a scrap of lace, and white lace at that, I have no doubt he can see the significant evidence of my arousal painted over the fabric and my thighs despite the lack of light. The white material is probably translucent at this point. I can't see his expression, but the room is so silent, it doesn't mask the way his chest bobs and breath rushes over his teeth. Even though I can't see him, I can feel his scrutiny as it roves over my exposed flesh.

"You're so fuckin' beautiful like this," Aiden whispers, the words raw like they've been ripped from his throat without permission.

I turn my face fully into the duvet, hoping it'll smother me before he forces me to face his punishment. The anticipation is almost worse than whatever he has in store.

"Why? Because I'm helpless and you're going to hurt me?"

"That'd be easy, wouldn't it? But no, that's not why." His fingers trail up the back of one thigh, and I quiver with the effort it takes to keep still. Another huffed breath. "I'm going to enjoy watching you figure it out."

"Psychopath. Just get it over with already. I know you want to, so stop playing—"

Smack.

The crack of his palm against my bare ass scatters my concentration, and tears sting the back of my throat, threatening to spill over my lashes. I breathe deeply to stem their flow, but my ass fucking stings. If I thought he would spare me any quarter, I'm sorely mistaken.

"Fuck," I whimper.

"Think you can take ten of these?" His palm soothes the sting, leaving a prickling sensation in its wake.

"Is that all?" I pant, but I'm lying my fucking ass off. "I can take whatever you've got to give."

"Fuckin' beautiful," he says under his breath. "You count them out for me, pet. Let me hear you."

I nod against the duvet, feeling a little disconnected from my body. He's mastered something inside me against my will. Reprogrammed something deep inside me to suit his needs.

Without warning, his hand comes down again on the opposite cheek, driving a sweet searing pain into me. I groan, my hips arching back, my clit needy and pulsing with an ache that demands satisfaction. I don't realize I'm grinding into his thighs, searching for friction until he wedges something solid, smooth, and warm with the heat of his body between his thigh and my pussy. "Count for me."

"T-two," I warble, then I clear my throat of the knot lodged there and say more solidly, "What is that? What did you do?"

"I said you'd get those six orgasms, but I didn't say when. You'll come when I let you. For now, you're going to take your punishment, and your sweet little clit will have to wait."

He punctuates this statement with another hard smack on my ass. My brain is so scrambled by the suddenness and the multiplication of the sting that it takes a minute for me to process what I'm feeling pressed between my body and the sweet friction of his muscular thigh.

Is that his...

It's his mask.

Aiden took off his fucking mask and arranged it sideways to cup my cunt like some demented chastity belt to limit sensation to my clit. Because an experimental twitch of my hips reveals I feel next to nothing grinding against its unforgiving surface. I don't know whether to be amused, offended, or pissed off, but he doesn't spare me a second to figure it out.

The next slap comes, followed by another two in rapid succession, switching from cheek to cheek. I forget everything I'm supposed to be feeling other than the constant threat of his palm. I bite into the duvet to keep from screaming—or begging—though I don't know which. He alternates, never hitting the same place twice, but each is more biting than the next, offering no relief.

I know how many times he's spanked me only because he's relentless about calling them out. By the time I moan out, "Eight," I'm willing to do almost anything for him to touch me, anywhere. I taste blood to keep from begging. Tears leak from the corners of my eyes and onto the fabric below me. His mask grinds into me, and I swear to God, maybe I don't even need his thigh. Perhaps I could come from this, from one hand driving bruises into my skin and the other kneading my ass, spreading it wide enough that I know there's not a damn thing I can hide from him. Until there's nothing I want to hide from him.

On the next, my hips tip up to meet the blow, and it causes him to connect lower, practically on my upturned cunt. I moan out my desperation into the duvet, shuddering as unfulfilled spasms wrack my body.

"Nine," comes a hoarse voice, and I'd be shocked to realize the voice is mine if I weren't going mad with the demanding, aching emptiness inside me.

"Keep still now."

I whimper, sucking at the fresh wound on the inside of my cheek, letting the blood coat my tongue, the bitterness distracting me from the impulse to snarl that he fuck me. My mask hangs on for dear life, and I can only hope the knot keeping it secure doesn't unravel as easily as I have.

It takes all my self-control, but I keep still for the last blow. Without a word, he maneuvers me from across his lap until I'm on my knees at his feet. My feet press into my stinging ass, and I suck in a breath. When I lift my eyes, I find him above me, mask and gun at his side, and his bare, handsome face staring down at me.

Greedily, I drink him in, committing it to memory. The reality of his punishment dulls for a second. Those gray eyes do the same to me, his thumbs coming up to collect my tears on the tips of his fingers, and then he rubs the moisture into his lips as though to drink them in. His brows, a few shades darker than his dirty-blond hair, lower as his gaze sweeps over me. Strong nose, angular cheekbones, a defined jaw. My hands ball into fists so I don't reach for him. We stare at each other for an eternity until I finally break, and my focus drops to his mouth. Even though his mask hadn't obscured his lips—his fucking mask—I've been thinking about what they'd taste like all night.

My pussy pulses, demanding attention, and my hips grind of their own accord, my ass pressing further into the heels of my feet for stimulation. One of his tattooed hands flies up and makes its home around my throat. My breath catches, and I realize too late that I've pressed forward into his grip, needing more of his touch, no matter its origin.

Aiden's free hand comes to cup my jaw. "I have promises to keep, don't I?" he murmurs. "Is that what you want? For me to make you come again?" His hand tightens on my throat until I have to stretch to keep my ability to breathe. Blood rushes into my face from how tightly he grips my neck. If I didn't still have my mask, I'd feel more exposed than I would if we were completely naked.

"Can I—" I nod to the undeniable heaviness between his thighs.

He tugs me impossibly closer and bends down until

our lips brush once, twice. "You want to put your mouth on it?" I sigh against his lips, but he evades my attempts to deepen it to a genuine kiss. "Tell me and I might let you." His voice comes again, softer now, a rasp in the semi-darkness. "Tell me you want it. Please. Give me the words."

It makes little sense. It's not rational. No amount of logic can explain why I look into his eyes and say, "I want to. Let me please."

His hand drops to his buckle. The clink of metal is followed by the rasp of his zipper. He fists his cock and draws it out of black briefs as his pants drop. "You do beg so pretty. Open your mouth and show me what a good girl you can be for me."

Aiden's praise fills me with liquid warmth, turning my tense muscles loose and pliant. I move closer between his spread thighs, studying him. His cock is thick and long, beautiful, and adorned with a piercing I can't identify in the low light.

I don't have time to be intimidated by his frankly shocking girth because he draws me inexorably forward. I automatically brace my hands on his thighs, opening my mouth to take him inside. When I suck the head, my tongue flicks out to investigate the piercing. It's heavy and foreign to my tongue, the metal clicking against my teeth.

A groan tears from his throat as I stroke and tease

him, and he flexes, driving deeper inside and triggering my gag reflex. I breathe through it, popping off and taking him in one hand as I flick my attention up to where he's staring down at me. I've always had a hard time giving head because I don't enjoy the sensation. He's so thick I can barely take him at all without discomfort, but he smells and tastes so good, I hold eye contact as I try my best to ruin him. His earthy scent floods my mouth, filling my nose. Tears stream from the corners of my eyes, and he knuckles them away.

Aiden's free hand finds its way to my hair, fisting it, but not to force himself any deeper. He uses it as though he needs to ground himself. The only sounds in the room are the lurid, wet slurps I make and the great bellows of his lungs as I finally get him to break his perfectly maintained composure. I draw off to take another breath and lick the underside of his cock, swirling my attention around the tip.

He shudders, thighs tensing around me. I do it again, and his fist tightens in my hair to the point of pain.

"What's wrong?" I ask with faux sincerity. The head of his cock rubs against my lips with every word. "Am I being too rough with you? Does it hurt? Do you want me to stop?"

Something shifts behind his eyes, or maybe there's the slightest softening of his face, an openness that wasn't present moments before. The tough, brutal man who'd murdered someone in cold blood right in front of me is gone, and the one left behind is staring down at me with liquid eyes, practically begging me to give him more.

"Or do you really want to come?"

He chuckles darkly. "You really are a brat," he almost snarls.

Instead of denying it, I suck him back inside, trying —and failing—to take him as deep as I'd like. My gag reflex and his girth simply don't allow it. He tries to choke out a denial, but his response cuts off with a moan. I free a hand to slip it down between my thighs. If he won't give me an orgasm, then I'll take one. I'm so wet, my fingers sink in easily, and I groan around him. My hips work, fucking myself, grinding my clit on the heel of my hand as I work his cock with my mouth.

Bliss.

Until he sucks a breath in through his nose and his fists tug me off again. He yanks me until I have to pull out my fingers and rest them on his knee to keep my balance. Evidence of my arousal coats his skin. His gorgeous cock bobs in front of me, and all I can think about is how empty I am and how much I want his delicious length inside me. Stretching me. Filling me. What I'd be willing to let him do to me to get it.

Noticing the sticky residue on his skin, he nods to it

and says, "Clean it up." My mouth drops open. I scoff in my throat, but he's already pressing my open mouth against his skin. A musky tang coats my tongue. I don't know why the fuck I find it hot, but I do. And I want his cock more than anything now, so I do as I amI'm told. I lick my salty arousal from his skin, enjoying the way his eyes glint with feverish desire.

"That's it," he whispers. "Get it all. That pussy is for me to enjoy tonight. You don't get to take it away from me. If you try that again, I'll edge you until you black out. Do you understand?"

When he deems it clean enough, he tugs my hair until my attention reluctantly shifts back up to his face. His hold urges me up to my feet. Without another word, he releases me as I stagger, and in seconds, he strips off my dress and rips my flimsy thong from my hips. The material bites into my skin, but I barely feel the sting. Then, I'm naked in front of him.

At his nod, I unbutton his dress shirt with trembling fingers before pushing it off his shoulders, baring his muscular chest and arms to my ravenous gaze. There's barely any skin visible beneath the multitude of tattoos. They paint nearly every inch of him from what I can see of his abdomen, all the way up to his throat. Skulls. Dragons. Flowers.

But I think my favorite is the death moth at the base of his throat.

All I want to do is kiss it, put my tongue to his skin there, and bite down until I can hear his hiss of pain.

Giving in to the impulse, I bend and press my lips to the ink, humming as his throat bobs underneath my mouth. Aiden only allows it for a second before he flips us on the bed, lifting me with a broad palm until he places my head on the pillows. He retrieves the pistol and pushes up to his knees over me. The dull black metal barely reflects any light, but I don't need to see it to know exactly what he's capable of.

Aiden seems to drink in the sight of my fear as he draws the barrel of the gun over my skin, his gaze flicking between its progress to my face to drink in my reaction. The metal is cold, with a rough edge, and it leaves thin red lines behind its track over my stomach, up my rib cage, and over the slopes of my breasts. My nipples pinch painfully in response to the stimulation, and his chest heaves as he draws the dull edge over their sensitive peaks.

"Do you like this?" he asks, circling the aching bud.

I fist my hands in the duvet to keep from moving, for fear I'll jerk, and he'll pull the trigger accidentally. I don't think he really would because I doubt it's even loaded. But the edge of fear is intoxicating, drenching me in conflicting emotions that end up leaving me feeling cross-faded in their aftermath. My hips lift under his weight as he hovers over me, searching for pressure.

"Of course not," I answer when I remember how to form words. But my response lacks the conviction to make believers out of either of us.

"You like it. I can see your heart racing in your throat. You're so wet for me, you're nearly dripping everywhere. You love I push you like this. That I make you a little afraid."

I'd jerk away, but the gun is at my throat now, and the memory of what he can do to another person as a bolt of fresh fear passes through me. Dammit, and arousal, too. "Aiden," I whisper, not able to tear my eyes from his. "What are you going to do?"

"Have you figured it out yet?" he asks instead of answering my question. He climbs off the bed, giving me time to contemplate his question, and strips off the rest of his clothes before he kneels between my boneless thighs. As he absentmindedly strokes his cock, letting the head of it bump against my clit, he watches me with heavy-lidded eyes. I hiss out a breath, trying to think clearly through the warring chemical responses happening inside my brain.

"Figured out what?"

"Why I enjoy doing these things to you." A statement, not a question.

I sneer. "Because you have a screw loose?"

Aiden leans back and picks up the gun again. My heart drops, and he must be able to read it on my face because he's manic with happiness. "I think we both do. Try again."

I think of him tilting his head at my suggestion to bet on tonight. How hard he'd been when he was getting me off during the party. The way his eyes had gone soft when I was on my knees for him. "Because I like it when you scare me." If it weren't nearly pitch black in the room, if I weren't drawn so taut with the need to come and he weren't so...him, nothing could have pulled those words out of me.

I reach up and tug him by the neck with one hand until he's close. With the other, I arrange the hand holding the gun until it's pressed against my weeping cunt. I may like it when he scares me, but after all that's happened tonight, I know he likes it when I don't back down. "Now you promised me orgasms. Are you going to give them to me, Aiden, or were you lying to me?"

# CHAPTER EIGHT

The cold metal slips inside me, the barest advancement, yet all my focus is centered on where it invades my body. Heavier than what I'm used to, less yielding, and significantly colder. It makes me hyperaware of how hot my skin is against its surface. Aiden grunts as he watches it slide in, then shoulders his way between my spread thighs for a closer view. One arm cups around my hip and braces underneath my ass as he slowly slides the barrel of the gun deeper.

Without the mask obscuring his face, there's no hiding the obsessive mania in his expression. "This is how you want me to make you come first? You want me to fuck you with my gun? I was wrong. You're not a good girl at all, are you? You're a very, very bad girl." His mouth hovers over my clit as he whispers the taunt at the shadowy space between my thighs.

I honestly hadn't thought it through when I'd teased him by putting the gun between my legs. All I could think about was punishing him like he was punishing me. Shocking him. My mom always told me that my constant need to prove other people wrong would get me into trouble one day, but I never thought it would be this much trouble.

"I don't think I can—" I start before he fuses his mouth to my clit and takes up a steady rhythm, thrusting in and out as much as the short barrel will allow. He proves me a liar as his tongue flicks back and forth over my center, and stars explode behind my eyes. My inner muscles clamp around the unforgiving metal, and he doesn't stop. The receding orgasm builds back with a vengeance and quickly rolls into a second, pulling tortured sounds from my chest.

When I come to, he's licking the shiny wetness from his lips, chasing every remnant like its something he's savoring. He lifts a wicked eyebrow. "You don't think you can what... come? Now who's the liar?"

"I hate you."

A chuckle. "Is that what you were screaming?"

Before I can scramble for a smart retort, he's gripping my hips and jerking me down the bed until my ass is against his thighs. With his right hand, he lines up the head of his cock—when the fuck did he put on a condom?—and then he's pushing in, stretching me to the boundaries of pain, and he's barely even inside me.

"Aiden," I whisper. Maybe I do scream it. It wouldn't surprise me.

"I love it when you call me that."

The look on his face... I can't parse it. Can't ascribe meaning to it through the maelstrom of sensations. Him driving inside me, the gun at the periphery of my awareness, the way this is so wrong but feels so fucking right. Is it tenderness in the infinitesimal upward curve of his lips? No, it can't be. Maybe it's humor. Derision. That would be more in line with the absolute hell he's put me through tonight. Like he's aware of some big joke I don't understand.

He thumbs my lower lip, the digit pushing inside until I taste his skin. I bite down, and the curve of his lips deepens at my show of aggression. His obvious delight makes me want to cover him in bruises. I've never been like this with anyone else. What is it about him that pulls these feelings out of me?

"Suck on it," he murmurs hoarsely.

I do without protest, and then I groan, pulling away. "God, why are you doing this?"

"Hmm, I like that, too. Keep saying it."

"Why? Because you like to pretend you're God?"

"No, because for as long as you're in my bed, I'll be the only man you worship. Now say it again like a good little slut."

"Don't call me that," I whimper as his thumb tips up my chin so he can nip at my throat.

"What? Slut?" He pushes in another inch. "Is that not what you are for me when you're not being a brat?"

"No!" I nearly growl. I try to think, but he's so big, all I can think about is how good it feels. Fuck. It shouldn't feel this good. I'll never be able to have sex again without thinking back to this moment. Comparing whomever I'm with to him. He's ruined me. "I-I'm not... Fuck, would you please—"

"Would I please what?" He shifts his weight to his knees so he can sit up to see all of me. My thighs wrap around his hips, trying to draw him deeper inside me, but of course, I'm no match for him. He barely even budges.

With the gun gripped loosely in his left hand, he lets the weight of the barrel drag along my stomach, then I freeze as it traces around my clit. His free hand holds my hip still so I can't move away from the stimulation of the cold metal against my steaming skin. My cunt flutters around his cock, greedy for more of him and inexplicably turned on by the threat, by his filthy words, and by his rock-solid self-control. If I weren't so desperate for him to move, to make me come again, I'd push him to the edge like I'd done with my mouth, but he's dictating what happens now, and I'm powerless to stop him.

The gun traces around where we're connected, and I've basically given up breathing. I could die like this, and I don't think one woman who gets to experience his cock would blame me. All I want is to draw him in deeper, feel him inside me, filling me with his overwhelming presence, but he seems content to take his time memorizing every part of my body. It's like he's cataloging every part of me in a mental file. He doesn't want to miss the slightest change in what he can see of my face.

"Is that turning you on?" I ask to keep myself from begging for more.

"What?"

"The gun. Is it because you like that you scare me, too?"

Aiden studies the space between my legs as he rubs the barrel over my clit, watching me jerk in response. My whole body is on fire, screaming, but he's patient. Nothing like the man who'd practically whimpered when I had him in my mouth.

I don't expect him to answer, but he places the gun on the bed beside us. He shoves another inch inside me, and I make a strangled sound in the back of my throat. I've never felt so consumed by another person. So seen.

But the most twisted part of it all is that I'm starting to see him, too.

Starting to see that he's pushing me, not because he wants to frighten me away, but it almost feels like he doesn't think I can take it. And goddammit, of course I need to prove him wrong. I'm not even sure it's a test I want to pass, but my pride won't let me back down from any of his challenges. The reward will either be the best thing I've ever experienced... or the worst.

"I do it to remind you why you should run far, far away from me." He slides in another inch. Fuck. Why are there so many fucking inches? I never thought I'd curse a big dick, but here we are. "And if I only have one night with you, then I'm going to keep you right where you are for as long as I can."

Rhythmic contractions pull him the smallest bit deeper, caused only by his admission—not that I'd ever admit that to anyone. I try to breathe through them, try to relax around the impossible invasion, but the more I attempt to slow my response, the more it veers wildly out of my control.

"Fuck, sweetheart, I'm barely inside you."

But not even his harsh whisper can stop the sweet, biting orgasm from rolling up through my belly, twisting sinuously through my muscles, and wringing me out until I'm pliant and permissive beneath him.

"That's right," he's saying when the ringing in my

ears subsides. "That's it. Such a good little slut for me. I want you to admit it. Tell me you are, and I'll fuck you so hard you won't be able to walk straight tomorrow."

"W-what?"

Aiden shoves himself inside me, one thick, delicious inch at a time, and even though I'm as wet as I can possibly be, it's still a struggle to take him. Pleasure and pain and fear and desire all intertwine until I can't tell them apart.

What is this man doing to me?

He's rocking now, shallow little thrusts that only give me a taste of what it could mean to have him fully sheathed inside me. Ruined. "Why? What? Why do you care?" He hits a spot that has me gasping. "Oh my God, Aiden, please."

"That's right, sweetheart. I'm your god, and you're my dirty little slut. Isn't that right?" He gives me one long thrust, and my back arches to make him fit, not that there's any way that's possible. Magicians must have crafted his piercing because it's unbelievably good. Mind-bending.

He presses his mouth against my throat, tasting my whimpers with another grunt. I roll my hips against him, aching to be closer, to have him all the way inside, but he's still resistant to my urging. Unwilling to go at my pace. Infuriatingly patient.

"I could force you to tell me, but you're going to give me what I want, aren't you? Like you were made for me. Now tell me what I want to hear, and I'll give that greedy pussy exactly what it deserves." Harsh words whispered into the shell of my ear send bolts of pleasure chasing down my spine, short-circuiting what's left of my resistance.

Angling my head so my jaw rubs against his, I breathe out, "I'm yours. I'm your dirty little slut, Aiden. I'm yours, I'm yours, I'm yours."

The last is said into his mouth as his lips fuse with mine. It's simple, sweeter than any of the depravity we've indulged in over the past several hours, but it's his kiss that devastates me more than anything else. It starts gently, even a little tentative, a contradiction to the brutal man I've come to know. The barest brushing of lips. The tenderness catches me by surprise.

My breath catches, and he uses it to his advantage, deepening the kiss, his tongue invading and tasting. Muscles that had been tense with anticipation or lingering apprehension loosen, liquefying underneath him. I reach for him, wrapping my arms around his shoulders, my hips hitching up to cradle his abdomen, allowing me to take him deeper.

He murmurs phrases that aren't English into my mouth, and I wish I'd taken my mother up on learning

*Gaelige Uladh.* The thought pops like a bubble as his body presses full length against mine. Hardness against softness. I meet his words with senseless whines, unable to control the responses he pulls out of me. Mindless.

Thoughtless.

The way I've been...never.

I've never felt like this before.

Never had every anxiety, every thought simply vanish from my brain.

I float on the feeling, letting it turn me languorous and blur the edges of the world around me until Aiden is the only thing left. He's saying something against my cheekbone, the words too low and guttural for me to comprehend. My body tightens around him, clasping him with my cunt, my legs, my arms.

"Why did you have to be so fuckin' perfect?" he wonders aloud, more to himself than to me. "Taking me so good. Can you handle a little more?"

I murmur something unintelligible. My mask tilts precariously on my face, slightly obscuring my vision. It's a miracle that it's still there, literally hanging on by a thread.

"Of course you can. You'll take it all, won't you? Take everything and give it back as good as you get. Fuckin' perfect," he repeats. "Stubborn. Beautiful. Even when you give me all those pretty tears. That's it. Take all of it. Let me in, sweetheart. Show me you're mine."

I don't let him in so much as he forces himself to fit. Stretches me until I want to cry with how full I am. Then he's licking the tears from my cheeks, and I realize I'm crying.

"Please" is the only word I remember how to say.

The next orgasm—the third? Fourth? I've lost count —rips into me as his teeth latch onto my nipple. That twinge of pain acts like gasoline to a flame, leading to an explosive orgasm that rolls into another almost immediately from the rhythmic clamp of my cunt around him inside me. I black out for a moment, the world turning dark, my vision wavering, my ears buzzing until all I can hear are my ragged breaths.

*La petite mort* indeed. I've never truly understood the French phrase for an orgasm—a little death—more clearly than I do as my vision clears and my hearing returns.

Aiden could find his own release quickly after, but naturally, he doesn't. When I devolve into tears and beg that he has to stop, he only slows his thrusts. Kisses fresh tears from my skin, then takes my mouth until I'm sighing against his lips. He tells me how beautiful I am, how good I feel, and soothes me when I tell him I can't take any more.

I die those little deaths a few more times, or maybe it's one long, rolling orgasm. I stop caring and can only cling to his shoulders, clinging on to my last remaining link to the living.

When he finally comes, his arms are wrapped around me again, holding me tight to his tense body. I have enough awareness to clasp him against me, one hand low on his back, one in the soft bristle of closely trimmed hair at the base of his skull. I hold him like I never want to let him revel in the way he shudders against me, body slick with sweat and fused to mine.

I keep him there for a long time, long enough that the sweat cools and our heartbeats slow to their normal rates. Eventually, he pushes up to relieve me of his weight, and I have to bite back my protest.

"Alright?" Aiden asks, his eyes flicking over me to assess.

All I can do is nod, and he dips his head to plant a kiss on my jaw. I wince as he pulls out because there isn't a part of me that doesn't ache. I lie in the middle of the bed, unable to move and wondering if I can die there when he returns from disposing of the condom.

He scoops me up into his arms like I don't weigh a thing and carries me to the shower, which is already running. After he tests the water and deems it safe, he tugs me under the spray in front of him, and I groan at the delicious heat as it rains down over me. There's a tugging at the back of my head and before I know it, the mask protecting my identity falls to the floor with an anticlimactic splash.

"You don't have to tell me who you are. But I want to see your face."

I'm frozen as he turns me around, waiting for him to recognize me, but the only emotion in his face is satisfaction.

Relief takes the starch out of my knees and I barely manage to hold myself upright, and Aiden chuckles when he notices. "All the fight worn out of you?" he asks as he lathers soap scented with vanilla all over my quaking body.

Has he really not recognized me? If he had, wouldn't he have said something.

"Momentarily," I admit, my voice a croak. "If you were trying to ensure I couldn't run away, you've succeeded. For now."

Maybe he doesn't watch the news. Or doesn't care about American politics.

"There's nowhere you could run where I wouldn't find you."

My wicked retort dies in my throat as his masterful hand moves between my legs. He lets the water rinse me before he uses a wet washcloth to clean the sensitive flesh there. I grip a handrail to stabilize as my weary thigh muscles threaten to go on strike. As though to emphasize his point, his devilish fingers bring me to another brutal climax in short order, not stopping until my legs threaten to collapse beneath me.

"Try to run now," he says with a smirk.

I glare back at him and snatch the washcloth away to give him the same treatment. At his lifted brow, I shove him under the water and slowly drag the soapy cloth over his heavily muscled body. It had been so dark in the bedroom that I hadn't been able to study him as closely as I would have liked, and this may be the only chance I ever get, so I take my time. He submits to me as I lose the washcloth and trail my hands over every part of him I can reach at least once. It almost feels like goodbye, and I tuck my chin under when that makes an ache roil in my belly.

Once we're clean and dry, he pulls me back to the bed. When I resist, glancing at the door, he shakes his head. "I said all night. Now come here."

Me from a few hours ago would have fought him. But in the dark where no one can see, where I'm safe knowing that I'll never see him again, I tuck my body against his, loving the way I fit right under his chin. He hitches my leg over his hip, and in no time, he slips into sleep with me wrapped safely in his arms.

It's 3 a.m. I haven't slept at all. Meanwhile, Aiden snores softly next to me, his lips slightly parted, his face soft and would be boyish if it weren't for the angular lines of his underlying bone structure. I should have left the moment I was certain he was dead to the world, but I can't seem to make myself move.

The clock on the bedside table ticks down the seconds, growing louder and louder until it drones in my skull like a second heartbeat. Sleeping was out of the question when I realized he'd passed out, and I know if I wait any longer, I'll give in to the rest I so desperately need. My muscles ache, heavy and limp with satisfaction, my head fuzzy with exhaustion, and my thoughts won't quit racing. Despite the weights practically hanging from my eyelids, I've kept myself conscious by sheer will alone.

Am I afraid of him? The question's plagued me since he settled heavily behind me, his arm banding around my waist and holding me to his naked body. Maybe I'll always be a little afraid of him. But right now, I'm more scared of what I might do if morning dawns and I'm still here. Seeing him soft with sleep was problem enough.

Maybe I fear he'll ask me to stay, and the words that come out of my mouth won't be the ones I want them to be. The ones I know I have to say to protect the tangled web of lies I've found myself in. Instead, I'd agree to anything he wants. Stay longer. That I won't be able to keep my mouth shut. That I'll tell him who I am and why I basically broke into his house and stole from him.

I can't risk it.

I can't.

*I can't.*

It shouldn't be this hard to leave when only hours ago, leaving was the only thing I wanted. I've known him for less than half a day. It should be impossible for him to have burrowed so completely beneath my skin, but somehow he has. Somehow, it feels like tearing a part of me away as I study his face for the last time.

Because it has to be the last time.

I can't risk running into him again or staying a moment longer. I won't even consider searching out his name after I leave for fear it'll somehow lead back to me. The last thing I need is for news of this debacle to get back to my father.

No, what I need is a clean break.

Fingers clenched in desperate fists in front of me, I count down from five or else I'll never get out of this bed. *Five.* Angular cheekbones. Full, soft lips. *Four.* A heavy brow over mist-colored eyes. *Three.* Tattoos covering nearly every inch of his perfect skin, all the way down his throat and chest. I could study them for a lifetime and never memorize them all properly. *Two.* If I could kiss him one more time, I would. I'd go back and throw myself at his feet the first time he asked.

*One.*

Without allowing a moment to second-guess myself, I roll away from Aiden, determined to keep my eyes averted. Like he's a black hole, and merely acknowledging him is all I'll need to do to be sucked in. I find my dress thrown over the foot of the bed and climb into it as quietly as possible. My shoes are a lost cause. I have no idea where the hell I left them, and I don't want to risk wasting time trying to find them. The most important thing is my purse with my mother's phone inside. The whole reason I found myself in this mess.

It's on a side table near the door where Aiden left it after my mad dash through the garage. It feels like so long ago. Like the person I was then is so vastly different from the woman I am now that I don't recognize her.

Focus.

Nabbing the purse, I move across the bedroom to the window where I know my drop to the ground will be the easiest. No shrubs or miscellaneous garden accents. It would be easier to leave through the door, but it's not a risk I'm willing to take. His friend may be there or one of his other associates.

It's there that I pause, looking back at where he's still sleeping in the bed.

There's so much I want to know about him. So many questions left unanswered.

But I'll have to be content to end things here.

Because he's dangerous, and I have no room in my life for more peril.

Even if they have a mouth made for sin, a body like a god, and the ability to read me like a book.

So as Halloween dawns, I make my getaway, determined to erase last night from my memory—despite knowing it'll be impossible.

# CHAPTER NINE

## AIDEN

"Tell me what you said to her," I demand, pressing the tip of my gun so hard into his forehead that it must leave a mark. Well, another one, considering his face is already bloody and bruised. My knuckles sting, reminding me why I rarely resort to using my hands. That's more Eamon's specialty.

The man at my feet snivels. Pathetic. If I weren't desperate, I would have put a bullet in his brain when he first started begging.

"I didn't say anything! The bitch bumped into me and spilled her drink all over my fucking suit. I swear! That's all that happened."

I backhand him with the gun still clutched in my gloved hand. Blood sprays from where it connects with his jaw. Eamon hovers over my shoulder and steps back without a change in his expression as the blood nearly paints his suit trousers. The garage wouldn't be my preferred location for messy work, but I didn't have time to move him to a more suitable location. Eamon bought a warehouse somewhere in town for this specific purpose, but it doesn't matter now.

"Fuck, man. Fuck. I didn't even do anything." Tears spill from his watery blue eyes, but unlike my pretty pet's, these just disgust me.

I press a button on my phone, and crystal-clear security footage plays. She fills the screen, and I'd look away if I could, but my gaze is glued to her. Something horrible squeezes in my chest. Like there's a massive weight on it. I know it's her, not only because she's wearing that short-as-fuck dress that shimmers like starlight, but because I'd gone back through the footage a half dozen times after I woke up and found my bed without her in it. I'd followed her progress throughout the party. Watched our tête-à-tête over and over until Eamon was begging me to stop torturing him with my moonin'.

The man kneeling in front of me is the only one who spoke to her before she did her disappearing act upstairs, and I found her. I've already surmised he has nothing to do with her disappearance, but I also didn't like how he fucking looked at her. Too familiar. Too greedy.

The scene replays on my phone with him

manspreading, so she's forced to turn sideways to slide by him. He's got a devil mask on, but it's not hard to read his posturing. Trying to intimidate her. Enjoying the way she squeezes around him and flicks worried glances his way. It's not until she accidentally spills her drink that his composure breaks.

I wired the house top to bottom before I moved in, so the cameras pick up the way he spits out, "Bitch," at her retreating figure. If she heard him, she didn't pay him any mind. Maybe that's what pissed him off more than the suit she ruined. Either way, I didn't waste any time tracking him down.

"Please, I'm sorry. I didn't mean anything by it. I'm sorry. Don't hurt me."

I can barely restrain my frown of disgust. I'd put her through much more torment, and even when she'd begged, one look in her eyes had nearly flayed me with the sheer volume of her defiance.

"That mask wasn't fooling anyone. I'd know who she was even with a bag over her head. You'd have to be an idiot not to recognize her. For fuck's sake, I've only been to a few country club events with her father, but even I'd recognize a body like that on—"

He was dead the moment he confirmed he knew who she was. The bullet screaming through his brain matter silences the rest of his pitiful pleading. Not soon enough, my skull throbs with a headache from all his crying.

No, we can't have some simpering gobshite running his mouth.

Eamon scowls. "I told you she was a problem. Fuckin' eejit."

"She's not a problem."

"I hate to break this to you, pal, but you just killed a man because he called her a bitch. If you look it up in the dictionary, that'd be the definition of a problem. If Cian ever found—"

"Cian won't find out a fuckin' thing if we both keep our mouths shut. Or do you need more demonstrations about what I'll do to anyone who can't?"

Eamon mimes zipping his lips. "What do you want me to do with this?" he asks, tipping his head toward the body.

I flick a glance over it dispassionately, then retrieve a gold pistole from my pocket and flick it in his direction. "Have them clean the library upstairs and the garage and get rid of both bodies."

Eamon catches the coin in midair with a heavy sigh. "It's best to forget about her."

"I know that."

"You had your fun, but anything more would be—"

"I grew up in the same world you did. I don't need you to explain the risks to me."

Eamon holds his hands in mock surrender, the gold pistol winking from his palm in the overhead lights. "Don't blame the messenger. Speaking of Cian, he left a message to meet him at the Emerald this afternoon."

*Shite.*

CIAN LYNCH IS A STALWART FIGURE, staring out of the massive wall of windows in my office that overlooks the bustle of the Emerald Isle. The scent of his cigar smoke coils around the room like a snake—thick, gray-blue, and stifling. It clings to my skin, slithers down my throat, and fills my lungs with a trepidation so sharp, I almost forget to breathe. It brings back old memories, as it always does, and my stomach heaves in a violent protest that I swallow down.

Had someone else found her identity? It's not impossible. A flight from Dublin to New Orleans is only about fourteen hours. All of this flits through my thoughts as I close the door behind me, drawing his attention. He turns, and I keep my face carefully blank, this time without the aid of a mask.

The ice clinks in the crystal tumbler as he lifts it to his lips and drains the remainder, his attention still on the crowds below. A benevolent leader? Not a chance.

"Cian. I wasn't aware you were coming," I say,

keeping my tone neutral. Controlled. Always controlled. "Would you like a room upstairs? The executive suite should be available for you."

He turns, lifting a brow and leaving his damp tumbler on my glossy oak desktop without a coaster. My fingers twitch at my sides.

"Was I supposed to clear my schedule with you, Aiden?" Cian asks, a thin blade of a smile splitting his even thinner lips underneath his salt-and-pepper facial hair.

Of course not. My stomach knots, but I show nothing. I'd let myself believe that crossing an ocean might loosen his grip on me.

Eamon was right.

I am a fuckin' eejit.

"Never mind that," he continues with a wave through the blue mist of smoke. "I'm here because I need you to do something for the family."

I'm numb, something I never thought I'd be in Cian's malevolent presence. There's always another job. Another body to bury. Another chain lashed around my neck, dragging me down. I'm covered in so many of them that there'll be no clawing my way out. Something I have no doubt he knows as well as I do.

I'd fought it, at first. But I soon learned that dealing with Cian is a lot like Newton's third law of motion: For every action, there's an equal but opposite reaction.

Each attempt at freedom only ends up with people I care about hurt.

"I need you to find Gallagher."

I blink, go completely still. "Senator Rory Gallagher?"

"The one and only. The remainder of his payment is due. The house was supposed to be a down payment on the ten million he owes me. You'll find him and get the remainder. Five million and not a penny less."

"And if he doesn't?"

"Well, he has some family, doesn't he? I'm certain you can get creative."

"Of course."

Cian sucks his teeth. "He has some valuable connections here in America I don't want to waste so the sooner the better. But I want you to make it clear to the man that I'm not to be trifled with. Either he pays in money or we have his blood."

I nod stiffly.

"I'll take that executive suite," Cian says as he ambles to the door, leaving the sweating glass of ice on my otherwise perfect desk.

"Of course," I repeat.

"Your mother sends her best."

I don't say anything.

It's been a long time since I moved from my frozen place near my desk. Long enough that the light coming through the windows has shifted direction. My joints creak as I fall into the chair and fire up my computer. Connecting to my home security network, I pull up the video from the night before, starting with the moment she arrived.

*Catriona Gallagher.*

My little pet is Senator Gallagher's daughter.

One night should have gotten her out of my system.

It should have rid myself the need to know her, feel her, taste her.

But it hasn't.

I may not be able to have her, but I'll hunt her down along with her father.

Because like I told her...

There's nowhere she can run where I won't find her.

## CATRIONA

"Is that black car following us?" I'd twist around to get a better look at the driver, my gold bracelets tinkling at the sudden movement, but I don't want to be too obvious. If I could get away with evasive maneuvers, I'd try, but the last thing I need is for SENATOR GALLAGHER'S DAUGHTER, ARRESTED ON TRAFFIC VIOLATIONS, to scroll across tonight's breaking news. Said senator would be less than pleased.

"Stop being so paranoid, Cat. No one's following us," my younger sister, Elizabeth, says as she flips down the passenger visor to reapply nude gloss to her pouty lips. I frown, certain that a car has been on our tail since we left my house, then glance in the rearview mirror. My best friend Yasmine meets my eyes, then rolls hers. She shrugs and glances covertly behind us, her tight black curls floating in the jets of air from the blasting heater.

"She's right. I don't think they are. They just turned at the light," Yasmine says.

"Thank you," I say as my fingers tap out an anxious rhythm on the steering wheel. She sends me a quizzical look, probably wondering what the hell is wrong with me, but she doesn't press when I give a subtle shake of my head.

Thankfully, Yasmine is a forgiving and discreet soul who has not only kept her mouth shut about my recent activities but also didn't say a word when I finally showed up the fateful morning after my truly idiotic plan went disturbingly awry.

And by awry, I mean I landed in the bed of a man with a dubious background, experienced the phenomenon of multiple orgasms, and left before he could wake up and realize I'd escaped. I seriously doubt any explanation I'd given him would've stopped him from putting those big hands around my pretty little neck. This time, probably not in a way I'd like.

I push thoughts of Aiden O'Connor from my mind. It's over. I'm never going to see him again, and I got what I wanted. There's nothing else to think about. Absolutely nothing at all. No reason he'd want to track me down.

Punish me.

*Nope.*

"Hello?" comes Elizabeth's singsong voice. She snaps her fingers for emphasis. Twisting in her seat, she flicks a look at us both. "Why did you two even make me come today if we're going to spend it driving around in circles? I'm starving, and you promised me you'd take me out for lunch since I couldn't hang out with Rue and Iris."

"What?" I ask, wiping my hands on the skirt of my pink long-sleeved wrap dress and blinking at the street signs even though I've lived in New Orleans my whole life. "I wanted you to come. I've barely seen you, and it's your freshman year at Tulane."

She works up a fleeting smile. It's not much, but at least she's trying. "I'm sorry, you're right. I don't mean to make you feel bad. We've both been busy." I swallow back my automatic rebuttal and cover my guilt. I should have been home. Should have made it a point to carve out time for her.

"You realize that is the third left turn you've made, right?" Yasmine interjects before I can panic wallow. "Who Dat is on Burgundy Street. Perhaps both of you should eat lunch before this turns into World War III, as you get hangry if you skip meals. So, let's focus on the road signs and use our nice words, okay?"

I swallow hard, and this time, when I study the rearview mirror, I'm looking past Yasmine's concerned face to the black car I could've sworn was tailing us since we left campus. Maybe Elizabeth is right, and I've just grown more paranoid. Hard not to after what happened the night before Halloween. And God knows Elizabeth won't want to hear anything once I mention our old house or its connection to our mother's death. So, I swallow back all the secrets I've been keeping, triple-check that there's no black car in traffic behind me, and white-knuckle it the rest of the way to the café.

During our meal, I think I've convinced them I'm totally fine—until Yasmine tugs on my elbow as we're walking out of the restaurant a couple of hours later. Elizabeth weaves down the sidewalk with her phone pressed to her ear, blithely chattering to someone on the other end. She spent most of the meal swiping through her phone and glaring at everyone. A tendril of guilt eats away at my stomach at the relief that swamps me at not having to pretend to be happy for her sake.

"Seriously, I wasn't going to ask questions because you came back in one piece, but you've been off ever since, and it's been months. You don't need to tell me what happened, but I need to know that you're okay."

Yasmine has been my friend since I transferred to St. John's Prep in third grade. We both shared an obsession with 2000s Usher, abhorred seafood (which was practically illegal in Louisiana), and agreed that purple was overrated, but we could share pink as our favorite color. I've never kept a secret from her in my life—let alone one so big I want to burst.

"I'm probably just being paranoid, like she said," I reply, tugging on her arm. "It's nothing. Too much time spent watching the news."

She resists my attempt to get her to move. "You hate the news, so I know you're lying. Tell me why you've been acting like the FBI is tracking you."

"It's probably not the FBI."

Her mouth falls open. "What the hell did you get into that night, Catriona? I thought you said everything was fine." She lowers her voice. "No one saw you... did they?"

"What do you mean by no one?"

"The more you talk, the more bullshit I smell. Hurry before Elizabeth realizes we're walking at a glacial pace and harasses us some more. I swear that girl has an attitude problem no number of beignets will fix."

To be fair, Yasmine had tried to talk me out of my plan that night. But once I got the idea in my head, there was nothing she could do. Because all I care about is learning the truth about my mother's death. The police say it was an accident...but I'm not so sure. I was convinced I could find clues at our old house—where she was found. The only problem? The Irish businessman—or at least that's what everyone *believes* he is—who bought it.

My plan to crash the charity masquerade celebrating the opening of his hotel and casino had been dumb, not that I'd admit it to Yasmine, who would probably say I told you so. No one was more surprised than I was when I caught his attention. I nearly dropped my champagne glass when we'd locked eyes across the room. If this had been a love story and not a tragedy, it would've made great TV.

I was supposed to go to the party, sneak away when no one was watching to find my mother's phone, and be in and out of the house before anyone noticed me. What I was not supposed to do was spend the night with him.

Then, sneak out before he woke up.

"I slept with him," I say, bracing myself for Yasmine's reaction.

She laughs—and I freeze in the middle of the sidewalk, because that's not the response I'd been expecting. Recriminations, maybe. But not laughter.

"Good one, girl. Please. You would have told me before now. I asked you a thousand times if something happened, and you told me of course not." She does a double take when she realizes I'm not next to her. There's a pause where her smile dies, and her brows draw together. "Catriona, c'mon. Tell me you didn't keep that from me. Be for real."

I can't force the lie out of my throat.

Her laughter trails off and her brown eyes grow serious. "Catriona?" Her voice wobbles.

Guilt swirls in my stomach. I've never kept anything from her for this long. For one, I'd been terrified to say anything at first, certain that Aiden was going to track me down. And then, because I didn't know what to say. How do I explain to her the things I saw? What I did? If anyone would understand, it would be her, but I didn't even know how to explain it to myself.

"It's why I've been a little paranoid. Turns out he's not just a billionaire, he's... I don't know, but at minimum a criminal."

"At minimum?" She turns in a tight circle, hands shoved in her curls, laughing uproariously. "And I thought sneaking into his house was crazy, but I swear to God you've gone off the rails since your—" She cuts herself off before she can finish the sentence. We both freeze for a second before she continues. "Maybe you deserve to be a little paranoid. He doesn't know who you are, does he?"

"No. I never told him my name. There's no way he can know who I was. I didn't talk to anyone else. Besides, I honestly think he's forgotten about me. I'm sure it's just anxiety."

She believes that lie a lot easier.

But I still watch my rearview the entire way home to make sure.

He didn't come looking for me. It's been months. The night we spent together must already be a distant memory for him. He probably doesn't even think about me.

But I couldn't have been more wrong.

Continue reading Aiden & Catriona's story in Until Death now!

ACKNOWLEDGMENTS

I have so many people to thank. Sometimes I simply don't know where to start. Just know if you've ever reached out to fangirl over my books, if you've ever attended a signing, or messaged me on socials / via email, etc, I've thought of you. This book wouldn't be here without you.

To every dark romance reader who blew *Toxic* up more than a year ago, I never would have had the courage to write more dark romance if it weren't for your messages and comments. If it weren't for for you reading and engaging and sharing *Toxic*, there are so many opportunities I never would have received.

So this book belongs, in part, to your support. Your enthusiasm. There's a teen girl writing for Fictionpress in 2005, wishing she could be an author who'd be blown away by the love you've shown the adult her. So thank you. From the bottom of my heart. This book is my smutty, twisted, love letter to each and every one of you.

To Amy Parsons, Virginia Tesi Carey, and Jenny Sims for reading the very rough versions of *Little Death* and whipping it into shape. I applaud you. I bow to you. Thank you for your attention to detail and encouragement.

To Alicia Winings. Girl. I don't know how I would have survived this without you. You are a star. From late night messages. To threatening me when I wouldn't stop working during my wedding day. Your comments on this book that were so insightful I can't imagine releasing another book without your feedback. I'm so grateful to everything that you do to make this process so easy and to have you in my life.

Grace Barr, thank you so much for not ignoring my DM on TikTok begging you for Irish translations and beta reading this at the last minute to make sure I didn't fuck it all up. I'm going to hold you to a get together the next time I make it to Ireland!

Same goes to Renita Lofton McKinney for her insightful feedback on future books in this series and thoughtful conversation about including Black characters in my work.

To Justine Bergman from JAB Design who worked her ass off to create this cover. I appreciate the hell out of you for treating my last minute cover change with kindness and understanding. You are incredibly talented and I am so fucking lucky to have the chance to work with you. You are a literal badass.

As always, my eternal love goes out to my Book Junkies and Street Team for being along for the ride!

Last, but certainly not least, to my husband (I can't believe I can say this!) Charlie, my daughters and family for their love and support. To my in laws who love and dote on my children and allow me time to make these books happen, I couldn't do it without you.

Thank you.

# ABOUT THE AUTHOR

 **Nicole Blanchard** is the New York Times and USA Today bestselling author of the TikTok-viral dark romance Toxic, a wildly addictive bestseller that has sold over 100,000 copies worldwide. Known for her morally gray antiheroes, off-the-charts heat, and jaw-dropping twists, Nicole's stories drag readers deep into love's darkest corners—where no one escapes unscarred.

When she's not crafting twisted love stories that break your heart and then heal it, you can find her soaking up beach sun with a glass of sweet tea, getting inked, or running a farm full of lovable misfit animals.

Visit her website www.authornicoleblanchard.com for more information or to subscribe to her newsletter for updates on sales and new releases.

facebook.com/authornicoleblanchard

instagram.com/authornicoleblanchard

amazon.com/Nicole-Blanchard

bookbub.com/authors/nicole-blanchard

goodreads.com/nicole_blanchard

pinterest.com/blanchardbooks

tiktok.com/@authornicoleblanchard

threads.com/@authornicoleblanchard

patreon.com/NicoleBlanchard

www.ingramcontent.com/pod-product-compliance
Lightning Source LLC
Chambersburg PA
CBHW040908010826
48978CB00013BB/1191